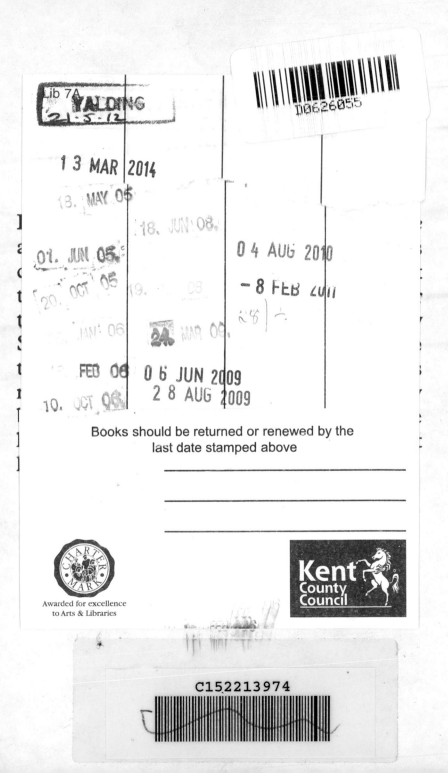

_____

_____

_____

A TOUCH OF MAGIC

In this sequel to *A Small Piece of Paradise* a boy, uncertain of his identity, tries desperately to adapt a life entirely different to that which he has been used to. After the tragic events in London's Sparrow Street, he and his donkey, Smokey, make their home in the country. But Joe is never completely happy, he feels he really belongs nowhere. Perhaps he could make his home with Ben——but would Ben want him?

A TOUCH OF MAGIC

A TOUCH
OF MAGIC

by

Geoffrey Morgan

Dales Large Print Books
Long Preston, North Yorkshire,
England.

British Library Cataloguing in Publication Data.

Morgan, Geoffrey
  A touch of magic.

A catalogue record for this book is
available from the British Library

ISBN 1-85389-636-5 pbk   C152213974

First published in Great Britain by Collins 1968

Published in Large Print May, 1996 by arrangement with
Geoffrey Morgan.

Dales Large Print is an imprint of
Library Magna Books Ltd.
Printed and bound in Great Britain by
T.J. Press (Padstow) Ltd., Cornwall, PL28 8RW.

For Sheila and Bob

CHAPTER 1

If you take the short cut across Prospect Meadow to Winkletye Lane you're sure to see Ben Pollard's house.

For one thing, it's the only place there. And if that's not enough, there's a notice to draw your attention: not a very smart notice, like you'd see in the town; just a piece of plain deal pinned to an elm stake on one side of the gateway, announcing free range eggs for sale.

Sometimes it has other things on it, too: strawberries, or cucumbers, lettuces or William pears, depending on the season. But it always has eggs. Even when Ben's hens are moulting or the pullets haven't come on lay. He gets them then from Brierley's Farm at the top of the lane, and any other available source. And you wouldn't know the difference because they're all fresh. But free range—well, that's another story, for the eggs from Brierley's are laid in batteries, and the range the birds get at the back of Ben's cottage is enclosed in two oblong strips of netting under the pear trees. The fowls have hardly room to stretch their legs let alone their wings, and the grass was picked off years ago.

Taken the year round, Ben's produce wouldn't keep him in beer and baccy, and although you could sometimes see him hedging or ditching on Brierley's land, and maybe in the fields come harvest time, the villagers reckoned he must have other means.

But Ben never talked about his means, not even in *The Crown* on Saturday night or when he went to church on Sundays. He kept his affairs to himself. He was an individual; not one of the herd. He lived alone, and was happy to be independent. But there was nothing of the recluse about him; no eccentric traits. He was invariably cheerful, always polite, with an easy, weatherbeaten smile for everyone. But he never made any close friendships—not in the village, anyway. In fact, he never seemed to have any friends at all. Until Joe came. And *he* came from London.

For Joe that meeting had been the entrance to a new and magical world; the world of the country and the wild creatures who lived there. For Ben lived close to the earth and close to Marley Wood that rose like a green shadow beyond his garden.

In London Joe had always reckoned he knew what the country would be like. But his reckoning was only the result of an occasional glimpse of it from an excursion train when Aunt Ethel and Uncle Bert had taken him and his sister Liz to Southend for the day. Of course, that was when he was very small, before Uncle Bert went to sea as steward on a cargo ship. In more recent times, Joe had found the nearest thing to the country in the garden behind the junkyard in Sparrow Street, where Mr Penny had lived. The garden had been more than just a green oasis in London's East End; it had provided a natural home for Joe's pets which he could never have kept in Aunt Ethel's flat. But it had been the Council's development plans and Mr Massiter's property company that had brought it all to an end. Oddly enough, it had been Mrs Massiter who had befriended them, and her vain efforts to save the house and garden had only finalised the rift between herself and her husband. Perhaps the distance between them wasn't quite so wide now, for the accident in which Mr Penny had died seemed to have changed Mr Massiter. But that was no comfort to Joe at the time, and with Mr Penny gone, and Aunt Ethel recuperating with the baby in Brighton and Uncle Bert in Australia, it seemed natural that he should accompany Mrs Massiter to her house in the country, where Mr Penny's donkey and all Joe's pets were awaiting them.

The new life at Valley End had done Joe no end of good. It had helped to soften the numbing blow of the tragic events in Sparrow Street, and the memories began to fade in the excitement of discovering a world that lay open to the sky.

But it was not until he met Ben Pollard that he became aware of the scents and rhythm of country life, the effect of the seasons on plant and animal, and the fascinating, thrilling and sometimes unpleasant sights Nature offered the experienced observer.

Ben had shown him some of these things since they had become friends. They had trekked deep into the wood in the spring moonlight to see the badgers at play, followed the tracks in the winter snow of the roe deer family, watched the woodpecker tap the bark, seen the fox set off the rabbit, the white owl dive for the shrew.

Joe found cruelty there as well as beauty. The way of the wild creatures was free, but danger lived with them in their freedom.

Despite his enthusiasm he frequently had doubts that he'd ever be like Ben—a true countryman. The trouble was he couldn't get used to the rawness of Nature. You had to be tough. You had to keep some happy creatures down if there were no natural predators to control their families, especially those that wrought damage on crops and trees. Ben was sensible about these things and accepted them. 'Ay, that be the way o' Nature,' he would declare when Joe protested. 'And there come occasions when man has to help Nature do her job.'

If he sometimes seemed hard, Joe knew he was kind, too. Ready to protect those creatures too young to protect and forage themselves; like the brood of mallard ducks he'd brought up in the spring, that still appeared for the corn when the hens were fed.

Getting to know Ben wasn't easy for most people. He wasn't too free with his confidence and his trust. Like all countrymen, he looked on strangers with a wary eye, especially the townee. But he hadn't looked at Joe like that; not after their first meeting. For Joe's youth, his interest and wonder seemed to have broken down the old man's cautious reserve almost at once. It could have been that. Or perhaps the large brown eyes and freckled face had something to do with it. Or again, maybe he was just reminded of another boy. Whatever it was, the man had taken to him from the first day he'd called.

And what a day that had been. For his arrival had coincided with a fiasco in the hen run and Joe had been able to help restore order by grabbing some of the fowls that were flapping about the garden. He'd come for eggs, and had ended up nursing half a dozen panicking hens.

Since then there had never been a time when Joe had approached Ben's cottage without a feeling of excitement and anticipation. Even though his visits were frequent enough—perhaps too frequent for Ben—he never felt the slightest qualm that there wouldn't be a welcome.

Never, that is, until now.

This morning was different. He'd got a

confession to make; some explaining to do; apologies to give. And not through any fault of his own. No wonder he couldn't appreciate the cloudless morning or smell the fresh scented clover as the sun dried the dew, or hear the larks singing happily over Highfield. And all on account of Uncle Bert—well, perhaps not so much Uncle Bert as his shipmate Larry.

They'd been in *The Crown* the night before and Larry had got excited and somehow there'd been a quarrel with Ben. Joe didn't know the gist of it, but as far as he could make out Larry had called Ben an old poacher and several other unpleasant names, and the scene had ended with a broken window in the Tap Room.

That was one thing. Another, was the bad news about Mr Massiter. Someone had rung from London to say he'd been taken ill and was in a nursing home. It seemed he was going to be all right, but Mrs Massiter had at once decided she must go to him, and she had driven off from Valley End soon after Uncle Bert's unexpected arrival.

Not that Arnold Massiter's illness had anything to do with Ben Pollard; but it did add to the confusion in Joe's mind because he would have to tell Mrs Massiter about the incident in the village when she returned. She'd be worried enough without having to consider the disgraceful behaviour of her two guests, who would never have been there at all if it hadn't been for Joe.

Joe felt it had been a bit of a nerve to call just like that, without any warning. True, Uncle Bert had a good reason; but to bring Larry with him just because they were on their way to Hull to join ship was too much of a cheek. But that's how it had been, and Mrs Massiter had invited them to stay the night. Later, they'd gone down to the village and there'd been the scene at *The Crown*.

And that wasn't all. Joe was still smarting from the discovery he'd made that morning after they'd gone. The small hard object wrapped in a paper bag under his arm was a further reminder of the shame he felt. A kind of trade mark that Larry had left behind of which Joe had to be rid.

Near the bottom of Prospect Meadow he threw the parcel into a tangle of nettles and heard it fall into the ditch. Getting the evidence out of the way brought some relief but it didn't make things any easier.

That was only part of the story he had to tell. He wondered how angry Ben would be, and he dreaded the thought that the old man could be so upset with the whole affair that when he knew Joe's own relation was mixed up in it, he might break their friendship and never welcome Joe to his house again. It wasn't surprising that the nearer he got to the cottage the more hesitant and apprehensive he became.

He climbed over the stile into Winkletye Lane, disturbing a pair of magpies picking grit from the road. A pigeon flapped noisily out of the elms and soared away towards Highfield. Then there was silence. A hushed expectant silence as if every living thing either side of the tree-lined lane held back with bated breath at his coming.

He walked on slowly towards the humped-back bridge and the quiet, scented air suddenly throbbed with a myriad tiny sounds again. Above the babble of the stream beneath the bridge he could hear the intermittent buzzing of a bumble bee, the rustle of a scuttling rabbit in the hedgerow, the distant cawing of rooks above the edge of Marley Wood. But there was no sound from the cottage.

From the bridge he could see the crooked chimney through the trees. A few steps farther and the gateway came into view. And so did the car, parked outside.

Joe hesitated again when he reached it. It was small, dark blue, a popular saloon you might see anywhere, but not usually as early as this in Winkletye Lane. If someone was after eggs then they must need them for breakfast for it was not yet eight o'clock.

He waited a few moments more and then as no one came out he decided to go in. He went up the wide brick path that edged the side of the cottage and paused by the water butt at the corner of the house. He could hear voices and he didn't want to break in if Ben was talking to a customer. He peered round the pink-washed wall to the back door. There was no one to be seen. And he couldn't hear the voices any more—only the sound of a blackbird scratching its feet on the corrugated iron roof of the packing shed. It was an old shed with patches along the bottom where the boards had rotted, but Joe knew it was light and dry inside for it contained the corn and meal bins for the fowls as well as egg trays, boxes, strawberry punnets and scales.

As he stood there watching, the blackbird suddenly screeched off in alarm and the partly opened door was pulled wide. Joe moved forward ready to greet Ben and the customer; but Ben wasn't there, and the two men who appeared didn't look at all like customers.

They were police.

CHAPTER 2

The appearance of the policemen shouldn't have frightened Joe. He'd done nothing wrong. It was just a bit of a shock suddenly seeing them there in Ben Pollard's garden.

Of course, he wouldn't have been so scared if P.C Fowler had been on his own—it might have been just a social call. But the sergeant didn't look the social type.

'Who is this boy?' he asked the constable when everyone had recovered from their surprise.

The village policeman smiled reassuringly at Joe.

'Joe's all right,' he said. 'I know him. Lives over at Valley End with Mrs Massiter.'

The sergeant nodded. His severe expression relaxed a little, but his steely grey eyes studied Joe's face as if searching for evidence.

'Looking for Pollard, are you?' he asked.

'Y-yes, sir.'

'So are we.'

Joe's knees began to knock. He suddenly thought of the trouble at *The Crown;* of Ben's involvement in it; of Uncle Bert and Larry on their way to Hull stopped by a police car. He thought this was the end of a grand friendship; and the pictures flashed across his mind like summer lightning—the court with them all in it and himself giving evidence. The disgrace that Mrs Massiter couldn't forgive; the final shame of being sent away from Valley End for ever.

He couldn't look the sergeant in the face. He stared at the ground, where a worm was wriggling from under a stone. That's what he felt like. A worm. And at that moment he wished he was. A worm couldn't answer questions and any second now the sergeant would start his interrogation.

But he didn't do that. He just looked at his watch, then nodded to Fowler.

'We'll come back,' he said. 'No knowing where Pollard is or how long he'll be.' He turned to Joe. 'If you're going to wait for him, boy, tell him we called and that we'll be here again at noon. Got that?'

'Yes, sir,' Joe murmured.

As they moved away, P.C Fowler patted Joe on the shoulder and gave him an understanding wink, and Joe felt a little better after that.

P.C Fowler was a good sort: kind and friendly; more like an ordinary person really than a policeman. He didn't neglect his duties, but he spent more time helping fallen characters up than taking their particulars down. He seemed to have been in the Force all his life, and in Elmbridge for most of it. He lived in the old police house at one end of the village, and his pride and joy was the garden that went with it. On the whole, he was very happy with his lot, and preferred raising prize-winning dahlias to winning sergeant's stripes.

He appeared to have a soft spot for Joe, which was more than could be said of the sergeant. He hadn't got a soft spot in him—at least, not that kind. He was probably soft where his belt went and under his double-chin; but inside he was tough. You could tell that by the way he spoke, the way he looked. Of course, he didn't come from Elmbridge. He was from the police station at Lotchford, which was an expanding market town that was creeping over agricultural land with its new overspill development from London. Perhaps life in the Force was tougher there. Perhaps he'd had trouble with some of the Londoners. If he'd guessed Joe was a Londoner, too, maybe that accounted for his attitude. Whatever it was Joe was glad to see him go, and didn't want to see him again.

Joe remained where they'd left him until he heard them drive away. Then he went over and closed the packing shed door to keep the sparrows from raiding the meal bins. He stood outside the shed for a while, his shoulders sagging, his knees still weak. He'd been lucky. If it hadn't been for P.C Fowler putting a word in for him, things might not have turned out so well. But they hadn't finished yet. They were coming back to see Ben. To make a case of it—what else? He wished Ben would hurry, although it was still a long way to noon.

He moved out of the shadow of the shed and sat on the edge of the cucumber frame. His knees felt stronger in the warmth of the sun; but the flies were a nuisance. The cucumber fame was on an old muck bed. Ben got the manure from Brierley's and brought it down the lane in his wheelbarrow. It was very good for cucumbers if you didn't mind the flies.

He got up again, hands in pockets, and ambled over the brick path to the fowl runs. He wondered where Ben was. He must have been gone for some time because he'd fed the hens before leaving. Joe could see the sand-like patches of wet mash lining the troughs which the hens were still busy picking clean. The troughs were old with rust patches underneath, but Ben kept them sweet inside. He'd made them out of old guttering, capping the rough edges with thin strips of tin to give a smooth finish to the sides. He'd made the water containers, too, by halving a five-gallon drum and turning over the edges. One stood in each run filled with fresh water each morning.

Ben was good at making things. He'd

built a wooden porch over the back door and had hung a big geranium in a basket under the eaves. He'd fixed a horseshoe knocker on the door and a new lock beneath the latch. Whenever he went out he left the key in the lavatory. Privy, Ben called it. Joe had never heard the name before, and he couldn't understand why Ben called it that even if it was outside; though, of course, being detached it did seem more private than one in the house.

He was looking at the place and wondering if the key was there now. He moved back along the path to the small wooden outbuilding close to the wall of the cottage. Ben had made this, too. The original privy had stood on its own down the garden. It was a long way to go on a wet night, and even if you did live close to the earth, there was no sense in being too primitive.

The place was strongly built of weatherboarding on an oak framework. It had a sloping roof covered with black felting, and a small hinged window on one side and a grille ventilator on the other. Ben had recently done it over with Solignum and it looked almost new.

Joe opened the door. Just inside was a

24

high, narrow shelf. There was a bottle of disinfectant there and an empty tin of Keating's Powder. Joe reached up and groped along the shelf. The key was there.

He closed the door, rolling the key over in his hand. Ben had told him to use the key if ever he, himself, was away. But Joe had never gone into the cottage on his own before. For one thing, he thought it a bit of a liberty. Another thought was that if ever anything was lost or mislaid, it might be embarrassing. On other occasions when he'd called and found Ben out, he'd gone away again and returned later. But this time it was different. He couldn't risk a moment's delay by leaving when Ben might appear any minute. And he didn't want to wait in the garden or the shed in case a customer called. He'd never served a customer before and he didn't want to start now with all he had on his mind. So he unlocked the back door and went in.

The kitchen was quite small and had a homely lived-in atmosphere about it. There were other atmospheres, too: the scent of black lead polish on the cooking range, the damp smell of wood around the sink, the odour of paraffin and the faint, stale air of tobacco.

The room was very neat in spite of the gluey flypaper hanging from the oil lamp. But Joe never saw many flies in the kitchen. He reckoned they couldn't get on with the atmosphere, so they stayed outside.

He closed the door and stood for a moment on the uneven brick floor. It was covered with coconut matting, but beneath the fibres he could feel the rough cement ridges where Ben had filled in the cracks. He crossed over and sat down facing the range. It was a huge affair and was the first thing that caught your eye, since it took up almost the whole side of the inner wall. High and black, it had a large oven on one side of the grate and a broad hob on the other where the black kettle stood. Above the fireplace was a metal hatch for cleaning the flue and, on either side, deep recesses where Ben warmed the plates or dried his socks. Over this ran a thick, blackened beam decorated with shiny horse brasses, and this supported a mantelpiece on which stood a Toby jug and three pint tankards, mellow with age. It was a proper dust trap when the fire was going, but you'd never see the dust unless you climbed on a chair, and then you'd be hitting your head on the ceiling beams.

Ben never had a fire in the summer. He used a paraffin stove for cooking and a Primus for boiling the kettle. He was so independent he wouldn't have running water or electricity. He reckoned the Water Board might slip fluoride in the water, and as for electricity...'Well,' he'd told Joe once when the boy had mentioned all the electrical gadgets at Valley End, 'with all them pylons and cables disgracing the countryside and exposed to the weather what d'you get for your money? Come thunder or snow, and what happens?'

'What happens?' Joe had asked.

'You're back to lamps and candles again, me boy. That's what. Any li'l burp from Nature and your man-made power's got indigestion. You gotta rely on yourself in the country, Joe, and no mistake.' He spat out of the kitchen window, it being wide open at the time. 'And all them boards and officials, too. Think what they charge you!'

Joe hadn't thought of what they charge you. Mrs Massiter paid the bills at Valley End. But he remembered the electricity going off once in a bad thunderstorm.

27

Then Mrs Massiter had been worried about the fridge, and Mrs Potter hadn't been able to use the washing machine and the hot water had gone tepid. Luckily, it hadn't happened at night because Mrs Massiter hadn't an oil lamp in the place. And Joe had never seen a candle there.

Ben always kept a packet of candles in the broom cupboard along with the hip bath and the hurricane lamp. He'd never had to use them though because he'd always got paraffin. And his lamps were always in working order and shone so you could see your face in them—just like the rest of the room. It all seemed to shine: the scrubbed deal table in the centre, the deep-shelved dark oak dresser with its brass hooks, the brass pump over the sink, and the glossy printed picture on the calendar on the pantry door.

Looking at the calendar he noticed that some dates had been ringed in pencil. He didn't remember seeing the marks before but that was probably because whenever he'd been in the kitchen he'd only had eyes for Ben. They were probably dates on which the more important customers were coming to collect orders. His eye wandered down to the slim pocket in the calender just before the dates. Overhanging the lip of the pocket was a yellow leaflet with some kind of announcement printed in red.

Joe got up and went over for a closer look, and he could see it was a handbill advertising Farrow's Travelling Fair. He thought it was an old announcement referring to the Whitsun holiday when the fair was last in Elmbridge; but when he pulled it out it was an advance notice of the fair's return in September.

He began to read it carefully...

All the fun
of
FARROW'S AUTUMN FAIR
& AMUSEMENTS
on
Spring Meadows, Elmbridge
(Elmbridge Flower Show)
DODG'EMS—ROUNDABOUTS
GHOST TRAIN—SKITTLE ALLEY
SHOOTING GALLERY
Don't Miss
THE CHIMPS' TEA PARTY
Sideshows for Everyone
SID FARROW'S FAMOUS FAIR
Note the Date:
September 13—For Three Days Only

Joe remembered the Dodg'ems and the Ghost Train at Whitsun; but the Chimps' Tea Party was something new. He wondered what kind of show that was. Chimpanzees! He'd want to have a shillingsworth of them. But it was no good thinking about the fair now. September was a long way off, and there were other things to think about in between.

He slipped the leaflet back into the pocket, and heard the grandfather clock in the front parlour chime the half-hour. As soon as the sound died another disturbed the silence. It wasn't easy to describe or identify the noise. But it came from upstairs.

He opened the door and stepped into the short passage connecting the kitchen with the parlour. About half-way along there was an opening in the wall. It was like another doorway without the door, and it opened on to the staircase. The light went up steeply, not more than a dozen stairs, the treads covered with a narrow layer of brown carpet.

He'd never been upstairs before. Ben had never invited him there. Not that there had ever been any reason. Ben was always up when Joe called and he'd never had a day's illness that put him in bed.

There was more than one sound now. Joe stood listening at the foot of the stairs. And he knew what the sounds were. He recognised the frantic flapping of small wings, then the slight thud followed by a scratching of tiny claws on glass. A bird had trapped itself in one of the bedrooms.

He ran up the stairs. At the top the highest stair became a small square landing. On either side a doorway faced each other, draped with nothing but a thick fawn curtain. He pushed aside one curtain and looked into the room. It was very small, with a heavy beam across it slung low from the sloping ceiling. There was a single bed, two chairs and a strip of matting. Nothing else. Overlooking the back garden was a small dormer window, and it was closed.

He turned his attention to the other room, stepping inside. And immediately saw the sparrow, perched on a corner of the chest of drawers. The little creature was watching Joe, and he could see the panic and exhaustion in the urgency of its breathing and the ruffled state of its feathers.

Joe began to talk softly to the bird as he moved slowly towards the chest. He murmured the same kind of encouraging endearments he often used on Smokey whenever the donkey was restless. But donkeys were different from birds. And, anyway, Smokey knew Joe. The sparrow had never seen him before, and before he could get near, it flew off into the mirror in the door of the wardrobe. Fluttering against the glass for a moment, it suddenly swept sideways and landed on the sill of the small window at the end of the room.

Joe advanced again but had to change course as the bird flew past him on to the bedside chair. In its panic it overbalanced and dipped to the floor getting caught up in the end of the linen quilt. Joe pounced then, and carefully scooped it up into his hand and carried it to the large sash window overlooking the lane.

After the first shrill squeak at Joe's touch the bird remained silent, watching him with its beady eyes, too petrified to move. Joe had been through it all before. He often found a bird trapped in his bedroom at Valley End. The creature had perched on his window and then flown into the room instead of the other way. They were nearly always sparrows, although once he'd caught a house martin there.

He pulled the upper sash down and put out his hand. Immediately he opened his fingers the bird took off. Dipping down over the lane and then up and over the hedge into Prospect Meadow.

It was following the flight of the sparrow that brought Joe's attention to the figures in the meadow. They were a long way off and moving slowly down towards the belt of willows fringing the stream, where Brierley's herd of Jersey cows were grazing.

Three, there were: three men. Two of them tall, the third short and stocky. They kept pausing on their way and looking around as if admiring the view, like holidaymakers; but Joe didn't think they could be on holiday because they were wearing bowler hats. And the shorter one was carrying what looked like a cluster of papers. As they seemed to be making towards the cows he wondered if they were inspectors—Government inspectors needing a closer look at the herd for some reason.

He followed their progress until they were screened from view by the hedge on the other side of the lane, then he pushed up the window leaving the gap from the top about where it had been before, and turned back into the room.

Ben's bedroom was the largest room in the house—the only one with two windows, anyway: the large sash window at the front and the small casement at the side. What furniture there was leaned slightly at an angle on the rough sloping boards of the floor. Huge brass knobs decorated the iron bedstead and over the rail hung a dark green dressing-gown. On the bedside table was a portable oil lamp, a Woolworth clock and a framed photograph. It was a portrait of a small boy. He looked a bit like Ben. Even a bit like Joe; but you couldn't be certain what he looked like really because the print had faded. It seemed so old that the white mount had deteriorated to a damp yellow.

Joe's attention strayed from the picture to the door on the other side of the marble-topped washstand. He guessed this opened into another room because you could see the small window from the garden; but you'd never have thought such a small cottage had three rooms upstairs. As he'd now seen so much of the house he might as well see the rest, although he reckoned the room was very tiny.

He went over and lifted the latch, but he couldn't open the door. It was locked. He tried again, but there was no doubt about it. He glanced over the furniture and then up at the pair of brass hooks in the thick wall beam, but there was no sign of a key.

He scratched the lobe of his ear which was burning a bit. It was funny really, when you thought about it. All the other rooms in the cottage were wide open and Ben went out and even left the back door undone sometimes; yet this door was locked.

Joe might have thought about it some more if the sound of a slow-moving car in the lane hadn't taken him hurriedly back to the front window. At first he was afraid it might be the police returning. Then he wondered if Ben had got a lift; but when the car came in view, it was much too big and official-looking for either of these two possibilities.

He watched it stop this side of the humped back bridge. It was a dark maroon colour with a special sort of badge next to the licence on the windscreen. The driver got out and stood by the open door peering through the hedge into Prospect Meadow. He wore a dark suit with a peaked cap and Joe reckoned he was a chauffeur.

The man casually returned to his seat and drove along the lane, slowing to a stop as he came abreast of the cottage. You could see he was a chauffeur for when he got out again he flicked a speck of bird lime off the bonnet with a duster as he stepped round the front of the car. He stuffed the duster in his pocket and stood reading Ben's notice. From there his glance wandered all over the house. He suddenly saw Joe at the window and put up his hand, and the next moment he was striding through the gateway.

Joe hurried downstairs, through the kitchen and out on to the garden path. He was in a bit of a panic. He'd meant to keep out of sight. He didn't feel like trying to deal with customers. But apart from that, he couldn't remember the price of the eggs or if there were any lettuces cut or whether the cucumbers were big enough. He'd just have to tell the chauffeur to come back later, that's all.

They met at the corner of the cottage, almost colliding as they skirted the water butt.

'G'morning, son,' the chauffeur said cheerily. 'You live here?'

'No, but my friend Ben Pollard does,' Joe said, surprised by the question.

'Is he in?'

'Er—no. Not just now.'

The chauffeur raised the peak of his cap a little and Joe could see where the band had marked his forehead.

'Well, perhaps you can help me.' He glanced back at the car. 'Can I get through to the main road again if I follow this lane?'

'Well, yes, but it's a long way round and a bit narrow. You go up to the top as far as Marley Wood then it turns left and runs alongside the trees and brings you out on the road the other side of the village.' Joe scratched his chin. 'But it'd be much quicker just to turn round and go back the way you came.'

The man nodded. He began to walk slowly back to the gate, Joe at his heels.

'Thought as much,' he said. 'But I got

to pick up me passengers over there.' He pointed across the meadow.

'I saw them,' Joe said.

'They're going as far as the wood.'

'I thought they were going to look at the cows.'

The chauffeur grinned, and shook his head.

'They're from the Ministry.'

Joe could think of only one Ministry.

'Agriculture?'

The man shook his head again.

'Town and Country Planning.'

'What are they planning over there, then?' Joe was very puzzled.

'Water supplies. For Lotchford. The whole area. It's all this London overspill. They're going to need more water when the place has been developed.' He moved on to the car, and Joe moved with him.

'But they wouldn't get much water from there. It's only a stream.'

The chauffeur grinned again.

'You don't understand, son. The valley's one of two possible sites for a reservoir.'

'A reservoir!' Joe was trying to grapple with the possibility. He couldn't imagine the valley any other way than how it was. 'D'you mean—they'd take the whole valley and flood it with water?'

The man got into the car. He wasn't very interested. He didn't live there.

'That's the intention, son,' he said.

CHAPTER 3

It was some moments after the car had gone before Joe moved. He felt quite numb. As if his blood was freezing. When it thawed a little he walked aimlessly round the back and across the garden to the stream that trickled along the boundary of Ben's property, the other side of the pear trees.

He stood, gazing into the clear water and trying to imagine what the valley would look like filled with it. Of course, it was a daft idea. He knew he shouldn't give it another thought. He had enough on his mind without adding to his burden. Still when you get a shock like that you couldn't help thinking about it, could you? And there were the men in the bowler hats to give it substance. You had to admit there were plenty of people with daft ideas, especially when they were in the Government.

But flooding the valley! That was the daftest idea of the lot. Think of the fields of corn that turned the slopes to gold each summer; the lush pastures that fed the cows and the sheep. No one with any sense would want to see it all at the bottom of a reservoir. And that was without counting Marley Wood and Brierley's Farm and Ben's cottage and the houses that edged down into the valley that were part of Elmbridge village. How could such a thing be done with all the wild creatures living there?

And what about the people? They'd be up in arms—especially the important people: Mrs Massiter for one. Then there was the Colonel. He'd have something to say. He lived in the Manor House. Colonel Clive Rawlins; retired, of course, but very much alive and active. They called him the Lord of the Manor. He had a lot of letters after his name, and a housekeeper and two servants and a groom for his horse. He called at Valley End sometimes and never took advantages because he was posh. He treated Joe like a real grown-up, and was quite friendly with everyone. Of course, that might be because he was chairman of the Horticultural Society and on the Council and several other things.

And what about Commander Lawson? Joe didn't know much about him except that he lived in the timbered house on the Lotchford road and his wife bred spaniels. He'd left the Navy recently and was something to do with the National Farmers' Union. He was an important person and Joe couldn't think that after all those years at sea he'd want to look out on a reservoir.

The doctor was important, too. You couldn't live without him. He had a large house with two acres and a wife with a horse and a daughter with a pony. He wouldn't want his acres waterlogged. And people had to take notice of doctors. People took notice of Mrs Chester-Smyth, too. She always wrote to the papers and her M.P when she had a grievance. She talked about it in the Women's Institute, and to anyone else who'd listen, though it was mostly her husband who did that. He'd been in the Air Force, but she owned Tudor House, and seemed to have most of the say.

The vicar couldn't be left out, either.

He'd shepherded the parish for ages, and Joe knew how much he cared for the valley because once when Mrs Massiter gave Joe a basket of flowers to take to the church for Miss Gunston (from the post office) to decorate the altar, the vicar had told him so. God had made the country beautiful; only men despoiled it. He was looking at the pylons beyond Monk's Hall at the time. But that's what Joe thought he'd said.

So the way Joe saw it he reckoned he needn't worry—not about the men in the bowler hats anyway. There was enough top brass in the village to defend the valley against any attack. And if that wasn't enough, there was the vicar, and he had God on his side.

Then there were the ordinary people who went to *The Crown,* who played darts and held meetings there. What would they be like if the inn was washed away?

Just at the moment, of course, Joe wished it was. For the mere thought of the inn brought him right back to his own personal problem. That was the one thing that was real and immediate. It set him walking again. Hands in his pockets, shoulders hunched, he looked for something that would ease his mind.

He followed the stream and crossed the weathered oak plank to the other side where just beyond the garden it broadened into a shallow pool. This was where the brood of mallard ducks Ben had brought up often spent their time diving and basking. There were ten in all. But none of them was there now. Only a moorhen, which scuttled with high squeaks of alarm into the tumble of blackthorn and elder overhanging the water on the far side.

He paused, searching the edges of the pool. Come to think of it, he hadn't seen the ducks for some days. They were quite big now, but Joe remembered the time they'd hatched out on Ben's old heap of straw, following their mother to the pool when only days old. They'd been a hungry lot, growing plump on the hens' corn, and always waddling over to the runs at feeding time.

They were wild, of course. They flew away. The large pond in Marley Wood was a quiet haunt for many birds and water fowl, and there was no doubt the mallards had made another home there. But Joe had never seen them fly. Perhaps because he hadn't been there at just the right moment.

Ducks usually took off in the early light of dawn or as dusk shaded the sky. Many was the time he'd seen them, geese on occasion, too, above Valley End or over Prospect Meadow, their necks outstretched in perfect line, their craking voices falling through the stillness of the oncoming night. He'd followed their flight into the misty evening shadow that spread upwards from the dark blur of Marley Wood, until they were part of the shadow themselves.

But the ducks he'd helped Ben bring up he didn't look upon as wild. He felt they were his pets, and at the time of their arrival they had made up something for the loss of his own when the fire had destroyed the barn at Valley End.

Joe wondered whether they were sunning themselves in the grass the other side of the blackthorn hedge, and was about to walk round the pool when the sound of a noisy engine in the lane halted him. He stood, listening, and realised the vehicle had stopped outside the cottage.

Three cars in the lane, and all in the hour! Who could it be this time? He ran back over the stream and across the garden to the water butt at the corner of the house. Remembering how the chauffeur had spotted him, he was more careful now.

The bulky wooden butt gave him good cover, although his view was restricted. But he could see most of the vehicle. A van. It looked small and old and the plain green paintwork was scarred with dents and scratches. The passenger door was narrow and didn't hinge back very far, which was awkward for getting out. So when it opened he couldn't see much of the passenger.

The boots came first; stout, brown ones, they were, then leather gaiters covering the calves of brown corduroy breeches, and then—but that was enough for Joe. He'd recognise the gaiters anywhere. Ben always wore them. Before the rest of the figure emerged, he hurried down the path to meet him.

When Ben stood up he made the van seem even smaller. He was tall, broad shouldered, with a straight back that belied his age, for when you got close you could see where the years had been in the creases of his face. His skin was taut, and tanned by wind and sun to the colour of mahogany, so you could tell he'd lived long and hard in the open air. His eyes were a deep blue, shaded by thick brows, and sometimes they narrowed coolly when following an animal track or watching the flight of a bird; but they were warm and wide when they looked at Joe.

'Didn't expect to find *you* here, Joe.' His voice was strong but gentle; rather like his hands which were big and brown, backed with fine dark hair. Hands which Joe had more than once witnessed dealing helpfully with a snared rabbit or a sick fowl with a firm but gentle persuasion.

'I came early,' Joe said.

'You been waiting long then?'

'Not so long.' Joe was looking at the young man who had left the driving seat and was moving round to join them. There was something familiar about the tight-fitting trousers and the T-shirt with the bright scarf loosely knotted round his neck in the style of a film cowboy.

'Joe, meet Charlie.' Ben introduced them.

'Hallo,' Joe said.

'Top 'o the morning to you, matey,' Charlie beamed. He had a thin, reedy sort of voice with a slight accent that came from somewhere Aldgate way. His face was narrow and pale, like chalk

46

when you looked at Ben's. His hair was dark and sleeked down with Brylcreem; there was a small scar under his ear and his mouth was thin but it looked better when he smiled on account of his even, white teeth. He was eyeing Joe with some interest. 'Seen you before, matey, ain't I?' he said.

'That's what I was thinking about you.' Joe remembered now. 'You're with the fair.'

'That's where it was.'

'On the Dodg'ems.'

'Right again, matey. Whitsun, wasn't it?' Charlie scratched his nose, frowning. 'Here, wasn't you with a woman?'

'Mrs Massiter was the lady,' Joe said. She'd gone with him to the fair, and when he didn't win a coconut she gave the showman five shillings to hand him one because Joe was disappointed. She rode the roundabout and the Ghost Train with him, but was dubious about the Dodg'ems. He wanted to go, so in the end she'd agreed, and Charlie jumped on the back of the cars and took the money. He rememberd it all now; but he didn't know Ben knew Charlie.

Charlie was looking at Joe and grinning.

'That lady o' yourn looked a bit of all right. Your aunt, I suppose?'

'No, not really,' Joe said.

'Joe's come this way for a bit from London,' Ben explained.

Charlie nodded. 'Very nice, too,' He grinned again. 'So like me you're letting your old folk fend for theirselves in the wicked city, eh?'

'He's on his own,' Ben said quietly.

'Oh.' Charlie glanced at Ben. He got the meaning. 'Oh, that's a bit o' bad luck, matey.' His voice was softer, the chirpiness had gone and there was a touch of sympathy in it.

Ben wanted to close the subject. Charlie was too inquisitive and he was sure Joe didn't fancy telling his life story.

He said, 'Let's be about your order, Charlie.' He began to move up the path. 'What were you wanting now—six dozen eggs—'

'Ten,' Charlie said as they followed him round the back. 'If you got 'em. And none o' them there battery ones, neither.' He chuckled. 'Got to give me customers the best.' He took a crumpled packet of cigarettes from his hip pocket and lit one. 'And don't forget the lettuce.'

48

'Five dozen, weren't it?' Ben entered the packing-shed and they crowded in behind him.

'Yep. That'll cover me for now. No strawberries yet, I s'ppose?'

Ben took one of the large wooden trays from the shelf. 'Not for a few days.' He moved to the door. 'Joe'll give you a hand with the eggs. I'll go and pull the lettuce.'

'Mind they're the 'earty ones,' Charlie called after him, winking at Joe.

They began packing the eggs. Charlie hadn't brought any boxes or egg trays so he borrowed some of Ben's. They were packed in trays of thirty in large wooden boxes with wired hinged lids. Charlie picked them out and handed them to Joe. He poked around for the brown ones, the largest he could find.

'So you're not goin' back to London, matey?' he asked, passing Joe a handful of eggs.

'No. My sister Liz and Aunt Ethel are in Brighton now.'

'Brighton, eh? Now, there's a plum of a place. You ain't livin' there, then?'

Joe didn't feel like talking; but he had to say something. He didn't want to be rude, especially if Charlie was a friend of Ben's.

'I lived with them in London,' he said quietly. 'Then my aunt had a baby and wasn't too well and they moved to Brighton, and there wasn't much room.' He paused, feeling a wave of sadness with the memories. 'Then—then—after the accident in Sparrow Street, I came down here with Mrs Massiter.'

Charlie came up slowly from the box.

'Here, hold on, matey,' he said. 'D'you say Sparrow Street? In Greenham borough?'

Joe nodded slowly.

'D'you mean—that crane accident—fell on a junkyard and killed the old man?'

Joe didn't say anything.

'Now—what was his name?... Ah, Penny, wasn't it? 'Course, I remember now. It was in all the papers. I was up North at the time. I saw your picture and the woman's, didn't I?'

Joe nodded again.

'Yeah, I remember the story.' His thin mouth was almost tender when he looked down at Joe. 'S'truth, matey, you've had some rotten luck. No wonder you don't want to go back to London. But Brighton—well, that's a different cup of tea. You'll be goin' back to your relatives there?'

'Not now I won't,' Joe said. 'They're going to Australia.'

Charlie sucked in his breath and clicked his tongue almost at the same time.

'Australia?' he repeated. 'Well, now, that's the *real* ticket. Plenty o' room there, and a chance to make your fortune. I'd go mesel' if it wasn't for me connections. Young country. Needs young people. You'd grow up well there, matey. Clean sweep. Start afresh.'

'I'm not going,' Joe said.

'You ain't?' Charlie's mouth fell open and he almost lost the cigarette end hanging to his lips.

'I like the country here. Though I don't like the school much,' he added.

'But Australia's full o' country.'

'P'raps it is, but I wouldn't want to leave Ben and Mrs Massiter. And I couldn't take Smokey.'

'Smokey? Who's he?' Charlie looked blank.

'My donkey.'

Charlie trod his cigarette end into the boarded floor and breathed two wisps of smoke from his nostrils.

51

'You'd find shoals of donkeys in Australia, matey.'

Joe was relieved to see Ben approaching. 'Not like Smokey, you wouldn't,' he said.

CHAPTER 4

When Charlie had gone they went into the kitchen. Ben took the bottle of methylated from the shelf and poured the spirit into the cup just below the burner of the Primus stove. He put a match to it, and while the spirit burned he filled the small kettle from the pump over the sink.

'Bright lad, is Charlie, but talks too much.' He pumped the stove until it roared with a bright blue flame, then placed the kettle over.

'I didn't know he was one of your customers,' Joe said. 'Never seen him here before.'

'When he comes it's usually early or late.' Ben slipped off his jacket and returned to the sink, splashing water into the bowl. 'Ay, Charlie moves around. Meets people. Him

being wi' the fair, d'you see?' He smiled.
'Makes a bit on the side, like. Kinda
middle-man, if you get me meaning. Takes
quite a bit o' me stuff. Puts his own price
on it, o' course.' He began washing his
hands. 'Can't blame him for that, though.
Got to look after himself in the winter.'

Joe was sure Charlie could look after
himself at any time. Not just in the winter.
And anyway, the winter was in the future.
It was the present that worried him, and
Charlie didn't figure in that. He stared at
Ben's broad back, listening to the rush of
water as Ben emptied the bowl. He didn't
know where or how to begin.

Ben took the first step. He turned,
rubbing his hands vigorously with the
towel, his eyes fixed on Joe with a warm
and faintly amused curiosity.

'Some maggot's eating you, me boy, and
no mistake. Soon as I see you I says to
meself, "Ben," I says, "that young friend
o' yours has gotta weight on his mind"
and I'd wager a cock pheasant you come
over here without breakfast.'

'I didn't feel like breakfast,' Joe said.

'There! Durn me—what did I say!' Ben
slipped the towel back on its peg. 'Well,
we'll soon put that to rights.' He opened

53

the pantry door. 'I've only had a mug o' coffee meself this morning.' He stood half in the pantry, looking at Joe. 'Now, what'll it be? Some flakes? Eggs? Bacon and mushrooms? Slice o' ham? Some o' each—or the lot?'

'I'm not hungry,' Joe said. He was too full of worry.

Ben stepped back into the kitchen.

'You can't get things in their right order wi' nothing in your belly, Joe,' he said solemnly. 'And if you're gonna rid your mind o' what's a-nagging it you'd best do so while we're eating.'

'Well—then—' Joe tried to think of food. 'P'raps I will have something.'

'O' course you will.'

'But not much.'

'You say it.'

'Well...' He thought some more. 'What about a honey sandwich?'

A honey sandwich it was. Ben got Joe to help himself while he cut a thick slice of ham and made the tea. But when they sat down to eat Joe couldn't hold back any longer. He had to come out with it before he could take a bite.

'The police were waiting when I got here,' he said.

'Police?' Ben hesitated for one moment, the fork with a chunk of ham on it poised between plate and mouth. Then he shrugged. 'Oh, ay, Fowler, I s'ppose, wanting a statement about some trouble at *The Crown* last night.' The fork continued it's journey.

'Well, that's what *I* thought.' Joe sighed, for there was some relief in the certainty of knowing why the police had called. 'But the sergeant was with him. They came in a car.'

'That's what *you* thought?' Ben had stopped chewing and was looking at his visitor with some surprise. 'How did you know o' the trouble last night, then?'

'The milkman was the first to tell me this morning,' Joe said. 'I thought I'd better come right over and—er—explain.'

'Explain?'

Joe gulped down the piece of honey sandwich that was sticking in his throat.

'Well—yes—you see, Uncle Bert and Larry went to *The Crown* last night.'

'Your Uncle Bert was in *The Crown—last night?*' Ben couldn't believe it. 'The one who's always at sea?'

'Yes—well, nearly always.' Joe knew he hadn't started right and was making a

55

worse mess of things; but he had to go on now. 'And—and Larry was the one who caused the trouble. Not Uncle Bert. Larry's his shipmate, you see?'

Ben frowned darkly.

'Ay, that were the name,' he said slowly. 'Larry. That'll be what his friend called him.'

Joe nodded. 'Uncle Bert's his friend.'

'Thin, fair-haired fella?'

Joe nodded again.

'So that's your Uncle Bert.' Ben seemed to be staring at a mental image of Joe's relative.

'And Larry's very big with a scar under his chin and a gold tooth,' Joe went on.

'Don't remember no gold tooth,' Ben said thoughtfully. 'But he's a rum fella, and no mistake. 'Specially with the drink inside him.' He stirred the big mug of tea, looking at Joe. 'But what were they doing in Elmbridge? Your Uncle Bert's ne'er come here to see you afore?'

'No. He didn't say he was coming neither. He'd been on leave in Brighton and was going back to sea with Larry from Hull.'

'Hull?' Ben reached for his jacket and drew an old briar pipe from the deep

56

pocket. 'Come outta his way a bit, didn't he?'

'Larry's got a car which he's selling in Hull.'

'Even so.'

'But the reason he called was on account of the news.'

'News?'

'He came to tell me they're going to Australia.'

'What—the ship they're sailing on d'ya mean?'

'Well—yes. But he meant moving there.'

'Emigrating, eh?' Ben's thick brows rose slightly as he packed his pipe with dark, pungent tobacco.

'Yes. That's what he said.'

'Durn me! That's kind o' sudden, ain't it?'

'I was surprised,' agreed Joe. 'But he said he'd been thinking about it a long time. He was in Australia last year, you see? In hospital. Broke his leg.'

'Did he now.' Ben started to light his pipe.

'He said he looked around and made inquiries. Now he's going back to make some more. If everything's OK, he's going to send for the family. He reckons Aunt

Ethel's health will be better in Australia, and it'll be fine for the baby. That's what Uncle Bert reckons.'

'And what about you and your sister—er—what's her name?'

'Liz.' Joe was watching the flare of the third match. It was always a job to get the pipe going. The tobacco was so coarse, the bowl of the pipe so big, and the stem so short, that every time the match flamed over it Joe was afraid Ben would singe the hairs in his nose.

'Is she excited about going?' Ben sucked and puffed and a great cloud of blue smoke drifted across the table swamping all the other scents in the kitchen with its arrogant smell.

'No, I don't think so.' Joe took his eyes off the smouldering pipe. 'I think she's got—er—someone in Brighton.'

'A fella, you mean?'

'Yes.'

'How do *you* feel about Australia, Joe?'

'I'm not going.'

'You're not?' Ben stared. 'You made up your mind quick. But have you any say in the matter?'

Joe knew that if it came to it he'd have plenty to say in the matter.

'Uncle Bert and Aunt Ethel wouldn't make me. Liz neither. It's up to us. She's got this fella and I s'ppose she'll be getting married. And I got Smokey—and you—and Mrs Massiter.' Joe smiled, his troubles hidden for a moment behind the three closest links in his life.

'And what does the good lady herself say about it?'

'Mrs Massiter?' Joe looked anxious again. 'She doesn't know yet. About that—or last night.'

Ben sucked hard at his pipe.

'Well, you needn't be a-worrying about last night, Joe,' he said soothingly. ' 'Course, it'll be a nine days' wonder in the village, then there'll be something else to gossip about. But it don't amount to nothing much.'

'The milkman said you were called a lot of names, and a window was smashed,' Joe said.

'Ay,' Ben nodded, reflectively. 'There was that, to be sure. But I s'ppose I shouldna have hit him.'

'You—hit him? Who? Larry?' Joe was surprised. 'So it was a real fight, then?'

'No. Nothing as tidy as that.' Ben pressed down the burning tobacco in the

59

bowl and stared at the grey ash on his finger. 'You see, Joe, he'd had a mite too much o' drink, and were defenceless, you might say. But getting out o' hand as to call for something drastic. As mebbe you know, me boy, Friday's not me night to go a-calling. Saturday, once a week is often enough for me. But last week Gosling's missus asks me for some lettuce and cucumber for this week-end as she had visitors a-coming. So last night I took 'em along.'

Ben paused, marshalling the facts in order of their occurrence, and Joe took the last gulp of lukewarm tea. He folded his arms on the table, anxiously watching the other's face.

'Late, it was,' Ben went on, puffing smoke again. 'There were a goodly crowd in the Tap Room—most o' them reg'lars, 'cept the two standing at the bar.

'Well, I goes up and Gosling pulls me a tankard and I lays me produce on the counter. I had it in me pockets, d'you see? Unwrapped, o' course. And as I takes it out, the big fella with the pint pot and the tot o' spirits beside him, is a-watching me.'

Joe could picture the scene, although

he'd only seen the Tap Room from the pavement. The boarded floor. The stained deal tables flanked by backless forms with benches along the walls. The short, mahogany counter and glass-lined shelves behind with the glossy showcard of a nice girl drinking cider. In the middle of the wall at the back, the curtained archway leading to the other bar and the private quarters. He wondered who the regulars might be. The milkman for sure. The roadman, probably, and the postman, and farm workers from Brierley's and Monk's Hall, and the brawny labourer from the builder's yard who dug the graves when people died. And up at the bar Uncle Bert, short and wiry, anxiously watching the hefty figure of Larry watching Ben.

Now that he was about to learn what happened, Joe really didn't want to listen, for he knew it was a shameful story. But Ben told it quietly, with compassion and understanding, and Joe heard every word...

It seemed that as soon as the landlord had gone with the lettuce and cucumber, Larry had tackled Ben about his deep pockets. Poacher's pockets, he'd called them, and he wanted to know if maybe

Ben could produce a rabbit to follow the lettuce. Or perhaps a pheasant or two. The titter that went round the room might have embarrassed Ben, but he'd said nothing. Not until Larry offered a drink. Then he spoke, politely refusing the offer, and suggesting that Larry would do well to show the same restraint. That really upset the applecart. Larry went off like a bird scarer in Brierley's pea field, and said a lot of nasty things about yokels and poachers, and finally threw the tot of spirits all over Ben's face.

Rum, it was. The one drink that Ben couldn't take. But whatever the kind, no one would want to take it that way, and his reaction had been natural. It had only been a light blow on the jaw, but Larry crumbled like a badly set blancmange, and Uncle Bert patiently acted as second. Ben was so sorry about it all, he'd stayed to help; but it didn't do any good. For when he went to leave a few minutes later, Larry threw his pint pot after him. He'd ducked, of course, but the tankard had gone through the big sash window.

You could imagine the panic. With Uncle Bert hustling his shipmate out to the car, and the landlord in a right state threatening to call the police. As things were, Ben thought staying to help further would aggravate the situation, so he'd left very quietly for home.

Joe had listened to the story without a sound or a movement. And now that he'd heard it all, he still couldn't speak. Nor move a muscle. Ben, on the other hand, was a calm and cool as one of his own cucumbers.

'That's all there was to it,' he said, tapping the ash from his pipe, which had long since gone cold, into an empty tobacco tin.

'It's a fine how-d'you-do.' Joe spoke at last, rising to his feet and going to the window and back. He leaned on the table. 'If the police make a case—well, look at the shame it'll cause you and Mrs Massiter! And all because of me.'

'Nonsense, me boy!' Ben slapped the table lightly. 'You can't be held responsible for your elders, even if you are related. So will you quit your worrying, Joe?'

Joe wished he *could* quit. In every other situation he would have taken Ben's advice, but this was different from any other situation. He sat down again.

'The sergeant said they'd be back at

63

noon,' he said miserably.

'Oh, ay.' Ben nodded. 'He's a rare one for routine, is the sergeant. You'd think he'd have more important affairs to spend his time on than broken windows.' He gave Joe a slow wink, which was a cheery signal to get at such a moment. 'There won't be no case, Joe, I'm sure o' that. Not when I've had a word with Gosling. I intended seeing him this morning, and that I will. We can set the matter to rights between us.'

'You really think you can?' The signal seemed to be working.

'Why not? All he needs is a bit o' glass.'

'I know. That's what Uncle Bert said. He was going back to see the landlord this morning to pay for the damage. Or make Larry pay. But it was on account of Larry they had to leave in a hurry.'

'D'you mean—they stayed the night—at Valley End?'

'Yes, but they didn't come to stay; only to call. It was Mrs Massiter who offered to put them up as she thought it was a long way to Hull. So it was settled, but they hadn't been in the place long when there was this 'phone call from London

64

about Mr Massiter.'

'What about him?'

'He's ill. In some nursing home.'

'Ah, me.' Ben tried to make the expression a sympathetic sound for Joe's sake; but from what he'd heard of Arnold Massiter he was not the kind of man to waste sympathy on. 'It'll be serious, then?'

'I don't know. They said he was going to be all right. But Mrs Massiter sent me down to the cottage to get the Potters, and she went off to London. That's why she doesn't know anything about Australia—or last night.'

'O' course.' Ben nodded. He wasn't thinking about Australia or last night at the moment. He was thinking about Mrs Massiter. If he had any respect for women at all, he had it for Mrs Massiter. He didn't know her well; to talk to, that is. They were on different planes, though you were never conscious of the difference in her presence. He could imagine the kind of woman she was, and if there had ever been any gaps in his imagination, Joe had long since filled them in. He hoped for her sake, and Joe's, she wouldn't go making a fool of herself in London.

But he didn't put this to Joe. Instead he said:

'So after she'd gone your pair o' shipmates went down to the village?'

'Well—it was Larry who wanted to go. I don't know what time they got back, but this morning as it was getting light, I heard voices below my window—well, one voice was Uncle Bert's, the other sounded like a kind of groaning.'

'Larry?' Ben's blue eyes twinkled with a mild amusement.

'Yes.' Joe nodded grimly. 'They were walking away from Smokey's stable—well, Uncle Bert was walking and Larry was leaning on him. I got dressed and hurried downstairs and met the milkman at the door. He said he knew the old car in the drive. It was outside *The Crown* last night. Then he told me about the broken window. I didn't stop to listen much, but ran to the stable to make sure Smokey was all right. When I got outside again I heard a lot of splashing and a spluttering noise. I went round to the garage and found Uncle Bert holding Larry's head under the standpipe.'

'Rum fella is Larry.' In spite of Joe's anguish and his own share of worry, Ben was unable to control the gush of laughter Joe's picture provoked. 'Good for Uncle Bert,' he went on. 'What had his shipmate done this time?'

'Been in the stable all night.' Joe continued solemnly. It must have seemed funny to Ben, but it didn't tickle Joe. It was more of a nightmare. He wouldn't want to go through it again, and it wasn't over yet. 'I asked Uncle Bert what the milkman meant and he told me Larry had made some trouble at the inn. He was going to see the landlord this morning; but as things turned out he thought it best to get away. He said he's send the compensation when he'd got Larry safely to Hull.'

'Your Uncle Bert will be meaning what he says, Joe, I'm sure o' that.' Ben's tones were almost as solemn as Joe's now. 'He'll be a-getting Larry to make amends soon as he's got the fella in his right senses. But what was he doing in the stable?'

'He'd been drinking again,' Joe said miserably. 'Don't you see, he's a thief, too!'

'He is?' Ben looked shocked. His eyebrows seemed to bristle. 'Durn me, if that ain't fair a rum 'un. How you meaning, then?'

'I found an empty bottle in the straw after they'd gone, when I went to give Smokey his breakfast.'

'What sort of bottle?'

'It said *Rum* on the label.'

'So he'd filched it from the house?'

'Where else? I saw the cabinet in the back room, where Mrs Massiter keeps the bottles. The door was open. I don't know how many bottles there were but he must have taken one.'

'Then slipped into the stable for fear someone might come a-lookin' for him.' Ben was nodding thoughtfully.

'And slept there.'

'Couldn't get back, I shouldn't wonder. What did you do wi' the bottle?'

'I wrapped it in an old bag and threw it in the ditch.' Joe's face reflected the anxiety he'd felt all morning, but it was even more pronounced now. 'He stole it, d'you see? And even if Uncle Bert sent any money to-day the postman doesn't come again till Monday. So what can I tell Mrs Massiter? She may find out soon as she gets back.'

'When will she be getting back?'

'I don't know. To-day, I s'ppose.'

'Will the Potters be knowing about this?'

'No. They weren't up. When they came down I told Mrs Potter I'd seen off Uncle Bert and had my breakfast, and was coming to see you.'

Ben nodded. 'Some good sense is what you've got, me boy. Which'll be more'n can be said for that varmint, Larry. He's put you in a right state o' mind, and no mistake.'

'I thought you'd be angry when you knew all about it,' Joe said softly. 'I dreaded telling you. But I've still got to tell Mrs Massiter, and I'm dreading that, too.'

'Listen, Joe.' Ben leaned across the table. 'You'll not be a-worrying no more on account o' me, as I been telling you all along. And take my advice and say nothing to Mrs Massiter—unless she asks. I shall be along to see Gosling this morning, so that shouldn't be bothering you neither. And as for the stolen bottle—well, I reckon we can settle that between us here and now? He got up and went to the dresser cupboard.

'You do? But how?' Joe was so surprised he got up too.

But Ben didn't answer. He opened the cupboard door, rummaged for a moment inside, then turned and held up a bottle. New, and unopened, it was. He held it carefully, blowing the dust off the label, but Joe could read it plain enough. *Rum.*

'We'll find a bit o' something to wrap this up and you can put it in Mrs Massiter's cabinet.' Ben stood the bottle on the table. 'And no one'll ever know the difference.' He turned, opening the dresser drawer.

'But—I can't take that. Its yours—it costs money—'

'Will you stop a-fussing, me boy, and just do as I say. It cost nothing. Not me, anyways.' Ben produced a large square of brown paper and wrapped the bottle into a parcel, disguising its shape. 'Tom Brierley give it me last Christmas. A present, d'you see?' He placed the parcel on the table, eyeing it from all angles before he was satisfied. 'Now, I canna bide the stuff, as I was telling you. You canna give a present back just 'cause you don't happen to fancy it, so I put it away in case it might come in handy some day. Couldn't be more handy than to-day now, could it?' He pushed the parcel into Joe's hands, and gave Joe's shoulder a gentle squeeze. 'Now, you'd better be on your way, and slip that bottle in its rightful place afore Mrs Massiter comes home.'

It wasn't until he was in Prospect Meadow again that Joe remembered the men in the bowler hats. He'd forgotten to tell Ben about them and the chauffeur, and who could wonder with all the other things they'd had to talk about? But he wished he'd remembered. Ben would have reassured him, just like he'd done over the whole shameful business.

He hugged the parcel to his chest for fear he should drop it, and hurried up the slope of the meadow. Ben was a great comforter—especially when you were in trouble, even if he himself was one of the victims of it. Although he was a bit rough and ready and very practical, he seemed to understand about things: about people, especially ordinary people; their feelings, their strength and weaknesses. Even weaknesses as wild as Larry's. Perhaps that was because he understood about animals, too. He was a little like Mr Penny when it came to understanding. Joe often thought about

71

Ben and his lost friend Mr Penny. Ben was really the exact opposite in build and looks and outward manner; but underneath the rugged exterior Joe reckoned there was the same streak of sentiment and kindness that had symbolised Mr Penny's life. That's what he reckoned. How else could you explain his way with animals? They didn't appear afraid in his presence, nor cower from his touch. He could even whistle down a partridge and coax a squirrel from the tree. Truly, there seemed some magical communication between them in which Joe hoped to share some day.

He had almost reached the meadow boundary where its high hedge flanked the road, when he heard the car. It slowed down into a lower gear and turned into the opening leading to Valley End drive. Was it an estate car? Mrs Massiter's car? Although he hadn't seen it he was anxious lest it was. He clung tightly to the parcel as he rapidly crossed the main road, his spirits falling at the same speed.

He entered the little lane that dissolved into the driveway of Valley End. It was short and narrow with a gradient of one-in-ten, and sheltered on either side by neatly trimmed hedges as far as the white posts of the five-bar gate, opening on to the asphalt drive. Although this small section of public high way was like a lane it was called The Drift. Joe didn't know why unless it was because the winter storms sometimes filled the hollow between the hedges with drifting snow.

Half-way up, on the sloping bank, stood the red brick cottage in which the Potters lived with their dog Bula. Only the dog was in residence now for Mr and Mrs Potter always stayed at Valley End when Mrs Massiter was away.

There was no sign of the dog when Joe passed. Not that he was looking for Bula. His eyes were focused on the rose-covered porch of the house and the estate car parked outside. It was so much like Mrs Massiter's car that he decided to slip off through the shrubbery to the back of the house in the hope of getting to the cabinet undetected.

As he moved through the gateway and then off the drive a voice called to him from the porch.

Joe stopped, turned, and stared. Then he smiled.

It was Colonel Rawlins.

73

CHAPTER 5

It was not usually the custom of Colonel Rawlins to call on neighbours in a car. He preferred to ride one of his hunters. But he'd brought along a saddle for Joe which would have been awkward to carry on a horse. His principal reason for the call, however, was not so much the delivery of the saddle as for a word with Mrs Massiter.

He didn't know the lady very well. No one did in Elmbridge. She could usually be seen in church on Sunday, but her appearance in the village at any other time was rare, except for the occasional coffee morning and cocktail party. Perhaps she hadn't been a permanent resident of Valley End long enough to feel the community had accepted her. Or maybe the break-up of her marriage and the publicity of subsequent events which had brought her from London to Elmbridge with the boy was still too raw within her to allow her taking part in social activities.

Whatever it was, she was too nice a person, too important a resident, to be left on the outside. He had persuaded her to become a member of the Horticultural Society, but she hadn't attended meetings. He'd have liked her on the ladies' committee and, with such a delightful garden, entering for the show, but his efforts had drawn little response. But he thought he knew now how to obtain her interest; through the boy she appeared to have adopted—through Joe; and his donkey. That was the reason for the saddle.

Although the word he wanted with Mrs Massiter that morning was only in part related to the flower show. Something far more important was on his mind; something that would not only contribute to the termination of the society, but would engulf the valley itself. The new and ominous threat in the offing was of major concern to everyone in the community, and in the light of it, it was imperative to rally every scrap of support. Particularly with residents of influence; and he considered Laura Massiter was in this category.

But he was disappointed when Mrs Potter opened the door. Mrs Massiter was away—in London. She didn't know when madam would be back.

Rawlins hesitated in the porch after the door had closed, wondering about the London visit. Was it to see her husband? He'd heard she went up on occasion. And Arnold Massiter had visited Valley End. Rawlins had met him there just before Christmas. He couldn't remember any tension between them then. Perhaps it was one of those civilized separations you read about in which the estranged partners remained good friends.

Not that he could understand how a man could let someone of the calibre of Laura Massiter go. She was, perhaps, no beauty, but her charm was irresistible with a nature overflowing with kindness and good sense. Of course, there were always two sides to the coin. You could never tell with people—particularly women. He remembered once in India... That was the moment he saw Joe.

He went out to the car and raised the rear window.

'I've a job for you, my boy,' he said.

'For *me,* sir?' Joe had always thought colonels were crusty old men. Especially when they'd retired. But Colonel Rawlins wasn't like that. He had a soft voice; not the military kind that barked at you. His face was thin, but still friendly, and his hair was silver grey and receded from his high forehead in shallow waves. He was very gentlemanly with his manners, too, so Joe always called him *Sir*.

'What sort of job?' He stood tightly clutching his parcel as he watched the Colonel take a small saddle from the floor of the estate car.

'Oh, I think you'll like it,' he smiled. 'And it will give your donkey some exercise. So I found this saddle for him—or rather the groom did. If I'm any judge it should suit him nicely.' He held it up for Joe to see. 'Where is he?'

'In the paddock.' Joe was very puzzled. As far as he knew Smokey had never carried a saddle before. Joe had sometimes ridden him bareback, but he didn't like to often because he thought it might be a strain. For Smokey, that is.

'You have a harness for him?' the Colonel said, tucking the saddle under his arm.

'Er—yes, his bridle's in the stable,' Joe said. 'But—what's the job, sir?'

'Well,' he smiled, 'better not keep you

in suspense, eh?' He rested the saddle on the floor of the car again. 'I thought you might like to help out on flower show day and also take part in the donkey race.'

'Donkey race?' Joe was getting excited.

'It's not certain yet; but if there are enough entries we shall include a gymkhana.'

'Gymkhana? You mean horses and ponies and jumping?'

'Well, I don't know that it'll run to horses. We're thinking more of youngsters with ponies.'

'But I thought it was just a flower show.'

'That's the main object of the exercise, of course, but we always have stalls and sideshows which bring in useful revenue. We thought a gymkhana might go down well this year, and someone suggested we include a donkey race. I don't know if there'll be many entries, but I naturally thought of you.'

'Well—thank you, sir.'

'And that's not all,' went on the Colonel, with a smile. 'I thought you might also help to earn the society some money.'

'How could I do that?'

'You'd have a pitch on the ground and

give rides to the children. After the race, I mean.'

'O' course.' Joe was thrilled. 'And if we won the race there'd be no end of them wanting to ride the winner.'

'And even if you didn't win I still think you could do a brisk trade.'

'Yes—I'm sure—if Smokey's not too tired.' Joe's sudden frown gave his face a solemn look. 'I don't know if all that exercise would be good for him. He's never been in a race or given rides and that sort of thing. I don't think he's ever had a saddle, though o' course he did work in London, pulling a cart.'

'I'd say he's had an easy time of it since you've been here,' Colonel Rawlins smiled. 'He'll be as keen as mustard once he's had some training. And you've plenty of time to develop him.' He picked up the saddle again. 'Come along. Let's go try him out.'

It was only then that Joe was conscious again of the parcel he was clutching. He felt an inward flash of panic with the thought that Mrs Massiter might return at any time.

He appealed to the Colonel, 'If you'll excuse me half-a-mo', sir. I just have to

79

take this parcel indoors.' And he began running towards the side of the house.

The Colonel watched him go, a sad little smile touching the corners of his mouth. Nice boy, Joe. Thoughtful. Mature for his years. It was good to get to know him a little more even if the intention in doing so was to get on the right side of Mrs Massiter. He might have had a boy like that himself if he'd played his cards right, but all he'd gone for was a good time and his freedom. He'd supped both to the full in his younger days and had seldom given a serious thought to settling down. It was only when you were getting on you saw in someone else's child what you yourself had missed. Of course, the boy had not yet lost his early background. His English was atrocious on occasion. But it had improved since their first meeting, and there was no doubt that under Laura Massiter's guidance he'd grow into a gentleman one day, if not an officer.

Joe wasn't gone long. It didn't take more than a few minutes to go in through the french windows, place the bottle in the cabinet, throw the wrappings in the dustbin and return to the drive under the same route. And he and the Colonel set off to the paddock via the stable.

Smokey was on the far side of the paddock, cropping the grass under the trees. It was cooler there, although the hot sun never troubled him; but the shoots were green and moist in the shade. Joe opened the gate and called. The donkey looked up instantly, and after a moment's hesitation ambled across to them.

'He's in very good shape,' Joe said, stroking the animal's shaggy neck. 'But I don't know about racing him.'

'H'm...' Colonel Rawlins ran his eye over the ample midriff. 'Nothing much wrong with him that exercise won't cure. A little overweight I'd say.' There was no objection from Smokey when he placed the saddle gently over his back. 'What do you feed him?'

'Oh, the usual ration. Oats and hay mostly. You know, for breakfast and supper. He likes a mangel now and then. Does his teeth good. Ben Pollard gets them for me from Brierley's. And I always keep a few lumps of sugar in my pocket.' Joe slipped the bridle on Smokey and tightened the straps.

'What about exercise, apart from his roaming the paddock here?' The Colonel

81

stood back watching Joe fix the reins.

'I take him for long walks regular, and sometimes I ride bareback, though, mind you, I don't think he's keen on having someone up there.'

'Has he ever thrown you?'

'Oh, no, sir. Smokey'd never do a thing like that.'

'Then I think he'll enjoy it all as much as you will, Joe.' He moved back, leaning on the gate. 'Get yourself seated.'

Joe hoisted himself into the saddle and settled comfortably, forgetting for a moment all the things that had troubled him that morning. The saddle made a lot of difference. He felt more secure; he liked the feel of the smooth leather, and with the stirrups to support his feet and the reins to hold he felt as if he were a part of Smokey. He didn't know what Smokey thought but the animal gave no sign of protest; he merely turned his head towards his rider as if expecting the signal to move.

'Does everything seem all right?' Joe asked.

'Indeed it does.' The Colonel nodded. 'Off you go.'

With a gentle prod of his heel and a flick of the reins Joe set Smokey going, walking at first and then, half-way round the paddock, breaking into a run, and then walking again.

Rawlins followed his progress from the gate to the eastern side of the three acre meadow. Beyond the low hedge forming this boundary the ground fell gently away and you could see between the trees the russet and grey roofs of the village and the square stone tower of the church. Beyond, set against the slope of the valley, the Tudor architecture of Monk's Hall sprawled its mellow timbers between windbreaks of elm and poplar.

The Raydons farmed there—almost a thousand acres, and they always provided the site for the show and fair on Spring Meadows. The meadows, divided by a low fence, were broad and level, their vivid green patched with yellow islands of buttercup. Come September and the flower show marquees would rise there like huge, elongated mushrooms just as they had done each September for so many years. A medley of noise and colour and people milling through the afternoon. And in the evening, the lights of the fair, blinking out from their gay awnings to the hurdy-gurdy blast of organ music, and the inviting cries of sideshow barkers.

The day brought a gay sparkle to the quiet country air. It was a refresher well earned after the toil of harvest, and through the shortening summer days it was looked upon by all in the district as the last and most important event before autumn set in.

Rawlins looked upon it in that way, too. It was the very spirit of the country. In it the stout independence of the country folk manifested itself. God knows, few such symbols of that independence remained to-day. The increasing power of Government and Local Authority was making irrevocable inroads into the freedom of the country, bulldozing its way over the landscape, the character and the heritage of its people. Industrial development, mechanisation, expansion of towns and villages were slowly eliminating the old crafts, the fairs, the shows and the markets that had been the cornerstone of country life for centuries.

It would be yet another tragedy if this should prove to be the case so far as Elmbridge was concerned. Although the show would certainly not be the most

84

important casualty of the threat hanging over them. For the threat was to the valley itself.

He wondered if Mrs Massiter had heard yet. There was nothing official although he knew the Ministry representatives were snooping around that morning. The site had yet to be decided and Wyanstone was as likely a preference as Elmbridge. Information had, of course, come through to the council and every member of the R.D.C and the parish council was against it. It was obvious that he would be appointed leader when it came to the fight. Already he was taking action.

Colonel Rawlins had never seen much action during his military career. Most of his engagements, although in distant corners of the world, had been chairborne. His ribbons hadn't come so much from action in the field as from long and efficient service in administrative departments, although his long experience in the War Office might stand him in good stead now as it had given him an insight into the Whitehall mentality.

He'd collected various Orders, but looking back, they didn't mean any more to him now than good conduct badges. It wasn't wholly his fault he hadn't had a very active career. He'd never led his troops anywhere, except as a subaltern in peace-time manoeuvres. It was ironic that the most important fight in which he was likely to engage as leader should come in his retirement.

His first action was the setting up of a support list of the most prominent and influential residents, and he placed Mrs Massiter high on the list. It was a pity about her husband; pity that he wasn't resident in the district, too. Arnold Massiter, powerful chairman of Winthrop Property Developments, would be of great influence in any defence in the fight of the People versus Authority. But he must be grateful for the names he could count on so far. As the owner of Valley End, Laura Massiter would be an important contributor to the cause, and he hoped she wouldn't be away too long. He wonderd if the boy would know...

It was this thought that brought the sudden realisation that Joe had completed his round and was now awaiting some comment. The Colonel jerked himself out of the mental cloud the view from the paddock gate had created, and stepped towards the pair in front of him.

'How did it go?

'I don't really know, sir. He didn't seem to mind walking with me on his back, but I'm not sure he liked running.' Joe smiled. 'I think he'd rather I run with him.' He slid out of the saddle. 'It's best to give him a rest before I have another go.' He put his arm around Smokey's neck and took a sugar cube from his pocket.

'I think he'll shape all right in your hands, Joe. You'll both be in good form come show day.'

'We'll do our best, sir.'

'It's settled, then. I'll tell Miss Thornton you'll be one of the entries and that you'll also be giving rides, eh?'

'Miss Thornton?' Joe was puzzled.

'Our secretary.'

'Oh, yes, sir.' Joe's frown melted into smiles. 'I reckon Mrs Massiter'll be surprised when she knows we're going to race,' he said.

'The news shouldn't be too unexpected, Joe. She seemed very interested when I mentioned last week that we might find a job for you. I'm hoping she will actively support the show herself, this year.'

'I'm sure she'd like to. P'raps I can talk to her. I managed to get her to the fair Whitsun.'

The Colonel smiled faintly.

'I was hoping to have a talk with her myself this morning,' he said.

'She's away just now.'

'Yes. Mrs Potter told me.'

'In London.'

'Just for the week-end?'

'I don't know. She went last night. Mr Massiter's ill.'

'I'm sorry to hear that.'

There was silence for a moment. Joe stared over Smokey's head across the paddock, catching the view the Colonel had let go a few moments before.

'You know—' he hesitated. 'You know they don't live together?'

The Colonel knew. He didn't quite know what to say, but he was compelled to say something. Eventually, he said, 'That is what I understood.'

Joe went on looking at the view.

'You know, I've often thought about it,' he murmured. 'And wondered if it was right. Should good things come from bad things?' He turned slowly, looking at the man. 'Should they, sir? Bad—sad things—like partings and—accidents?'

'I think that's a question the vicar is more qualified to answer.' Rawlins had been caught with his guard down. He didn't quite know what Joe was getting at, and he considered it indelicate, to say the least, to be drawn into a question and answer conversation that might concern the marital relationship of the Massiters, particularly when the boy was living with one of them.

But Joe reckoned that if Colonel Rawlins could read the lessons at the morning service he was as good as the vicar for answering things, and after pausing he said, 'I thought you'd know, sir.'

'Well—er—I suppose there's a logical reason for everything somewhere, though it's not always apparent at the time. Misfortunes of some appear to bring fortunes to others on occasion. It's an ill wind that doesn't blow somebody some good sometimes, though whether that somebody is happy in the circumstances is another question.'

'That's it.' Joe looked as if his conscience was pricking him. 'I'm so happy here. But if it hadn't been for them—parting—and then—losing my friend Mr Penny, I don't s'ppose I'd ever have come to Valley End.'

'It's different for you, Joe. You're young. You've no right to spoil all that's come to you by dwelling on the past. You've all your future ahead. I'm not doubting you deserve your happiness. And there's the happiness you bring others.'

'I do?' Joe was surprised.

'Of course. Mrs Massiter, for instance.'

'I hope so. She's very good.' He was silent for a moment and then: 'You know what happened, sir, to my friend, Mr Penny?'

'I read about it.'

'Yes, it was in all the papers. It seemed to change Mr Massiter a bit.'

Colonel Rawlins was curious.

'Change him?' he repeated. 'In what way?'

'Well—' Joe hesitated, wondering if he was telling too much, but the Colonel looked so interested and his expression so warm, he felt bound to go on. 'He seemed more friendly. Had more time, if you know what I mean. He came down here specially to tell us how sorry he was about Mr Penny. He'd altered the plans of the new buildings he was putting up in Sparrow Street, so as to keep the garden Mr Penny had made. He sent Mrs Massiter flowers at Christmas and gave me a bike for my birthday. Things like that. He's been down two or three times, too, just to see if there's anything we want. You see, before it happened he didn't seem to care about anything but—well, money.'

'He's a very successful business man, Joe. They don't have too much time.'

'Yes, I know. But he's made time now. When I lost the pets I'd brought from Sparrow Street in the barn fire, he even sent me some field glasses because he knew I went out with Ben Pollard to watch the animals in Marley Wood.' Joe paused, then added as an afterthought, 'So I hope he's not too ill.'

The Colonel nodded. He seemed to hope so, too.

'I didn't know you'd lost your pets in that fire, Joe,' he said. 'Didn't any escape?'

'I don't really know. I think the weasel might have done and the squirrel, but the rabbits and the guinea pigs died. But if

Tinker and Nutmeg got away, I've never been able to find them. You see, I was away that week-end, at Brighton, seeing Aunt Ethel.'

'She's your nearest relative?'

'Yes, but she won't be near very long. She's going to Australia.'

The Colonel smiled.

'But you're not, eh? You're going to stay on with Mrs Massiter?'

'I hope so, sir,' Joe said. 'I wouldn't want to leave the valley.'

Rawlins wouldn't want to leave the valley either. Neither would he want to see it drowned in a reservoir. He was determined on both these issues. He moved back to the gate.

'I think you can take him another round,' he said. 'And you might ask Mrs Massiter to telephone me when she returns.'

When Colonel Rawlins had gone, Joe took Smokey another round, then put the saddle and harness in the stable. He decided he would go and tell Ben the news about the donkey race that afternoon. Despite the excitement that Colonel Rawlins had stirred in him he was still very concerned about the trouble at the inn, and he was anxious to know how Ben had got on with the landlord. He wondered about the police, too, and whether they'd been satisfied. Once he knew it was going to be all right, he would spring the news on Ben and get his advice on Smokey's training. Ben would know the best way of going about it, the feeding and the proper routine and that kind of thing. He'd know how to get a donkey in the pink of condition, and already Joe could see Smokey with the winning rosette.

Joe was still dreaming in the stable when Mrs Potter called him for lunch. She reminded him about washing his hands and when he entered the dining-room Mr Potter was bringing hot plates from the kitchen. Mrs Potter was old-fashioned, and wouldn't use the electrically heated serving wagon when Mrs Massiter was away. So Joe followed Mr Potter back into the kitchen for the gravy and the vegetable dishes. Mrs Potter came last with the chops. They all sat down but before she started serving she told them that Mrs Massiter had just telephoned.

'Well, Emily,' Mr Potter said in the soft, affectionate tones he always reserved for his wife, 'what's the news from London?'

'Mr Massiter's getting on right well, she says. He reckons to be out in a few days. All he needs, it seems, is a good long rest, somewhere quiet.'

'He won't be fancying that, I shouldn't wonder,' Mr Potter said.

'Well, then, he'll be putting up with it if it's doctor's orders.'

'When's Mrs Massiter coming back?' Joe asked.

'She doesn't know exactly, but it won't be till next week.' Mrs Potter smiled. 'She hopes you'll be coming to church with me in the morning, Joe. She says to tell you your new white shirts are in the airing cupboard.'

'So she's staying up there, then?' Mr Potter murmured.

'Seems like it.' His wife began serving the chops. 'She's going to ring again on Monday.'

Although he wasn't keen on going to church with Mrs Potter, Joe didn't say anything. He was very pleased really—about Mrs Massiter not coming back till next week. He thought that by next week the trouble at *The Crown* would have blown over.

CHAPTER 6

Ben was cooking a rice pudding when Joe got there. He usually baked one on Saturday and had it cold on Sunday after morning service. It saved a lot of time and slipped down easily with prunes or sliced peaches following the cold meat and potatoes baked in their jackets. Joe liked the rice puddings, too, and they'd often finished what remained in the dish when they'd been out together on a Monday evening.

But he wasn't interested now in what Ben had in the oven. He was looking at Ben's face, trying to trace some signal that might present a clue as to the outcome of his errand to the village that morning, and the visit of the police at noon. If a smile was anything to go by, it must be all right; but you couldn't always tell with Ben. His feelings didn't show much in his face. The skin was so tough and weatherbeaten they probably couldn't get through. His eyes, though, were different.

95

And when a smile beamed in them, you could read the message. There was a bit of a beam in them now when he looked at Joe.

'I been expecting you.' Ben turned out the Primus and poured the kettle of boiling water into the bowl in the sink, adding a little cold from the pump. 'This minute finished a bit o' grub, so you'll be in time to dry the dishes.' He tossed over a tea towel. 'Mrs Massiter back?'

'No. She 'phoned up.' Joe stepped to the draining board and picked up a wet plate. 'She's not coming back till next week. He's getting better.'

'Well, that'll be one thing we know. And you tidied things up at the house?'

'Yes. Oh yes, thanks. I managed it fine. But how did you get on?'

'I was about to be telling you.' His smile broadened. 'It's all been settled.'

'What did you do?'

'Nothin' to speak of. Gosling told me your Uncle Bert left him a coupla pounds for the damage, on account-like. And I says as how the fella wi' him didn't really mean what he'd done and they'd be sending full compensation next week.'

'And he wasn't angry?' Joe put a dried

plate carefully in its place on the dresser.

'Not so you'd notice. He hopes to get the new window in to-day.'

'What about the police?'

'Taking no further action, as they say.' Ben swirled the dirty water round the bowl and tipped it into the waste pipe.

'So it's all right then?'

'Just as I says.'

'So long as Uncle Bert makes Larry pay and sends the compensation.' Joe was unconsciously rubbing a dish with the tea towel as if he was polishing a piece of harness. 'We won't know till Monday.'

'I reckon your Uncle Bert's a man o' his word, Joe. You'll see.' Ben dried his hands and crossed to the mantelpiece for his pipe. He stood, filling it, in front of the range.

'Well, he's always kept a promise when he's made one. I know that.' Joe took a deep breath and the sigh that followed quivered with unbounded relief. He leaned against the table and watched Ben filling his pipe. 'I feel a lot better now,' he said, and added with a sly smile, 'I'll be able to concentrate on the donkey race.'

'Eh?' Ben glanced up over the flaming match. 'Donkey race?'

'When I got back to the house this morning Colonel Rawlins was there. He'd brought a saddle for Smokey.' Joe sat on the edge of the table swinging his legs while he told Ben all about it, right up to the moment he'd tried out the saddle riding around the paddock.

'Well, that's a fine thing,' Ben murmured when Joe at last stopped talking. 'Should liven up the afternoon a treat if the weather's right. And that moke of yours now, I reckon he'll just romp home wi' you on his back.'

'You really think so?'

'I do that. Fine li'l beast you got there, and no mistake. Always thought you should make more use o' him.' Ben sucked at his pipe, getting the last draws from the burnt tobacco. 'Strong, healthy, mature. You've only got to get him ready for it.'

'That's where I thought you'd help—you know, with the training.'

'That'll come easy. Exercise him afore he has all his grub, so he'll get to know he's got something to take to when he's done his stint. Then, nearer the day, you'll need to change his ration. He'll want something special—some beans and chaff, mebbe a bit o' corn and a good bran mash, to give him more strength and energy. I'll guide you about that.' He glanced at the calendar. 'But there'll be time enough.'

'Not too much time,' Joe said.

'A proper routine's the main thing,' Ben went on. 'We'll settle on something between us. But meantime you'll do well to get him used to the exercise.' He tapped out his pipe and glanced at the window. 'And talking of exercise—there'll be a job awaiting me now. I'd best get to it.'

'What's the job?' Joe slipped off the table.

'Moving them fowl runs. Got a piece of fresh ground that'll suit a treat. It's time they was off that ground. It's right fowl sick.' He put his pipe on the mantelpiece. 'If you've nothing better to do wi' yourself this afternoon, Joe, you could give me a hand.'

They went outside then, into the sunshine, and although there was a ribbon of dark cloud saddening the sky above Steeple Green, Joe was very happy.

It began to rain that night when he was going to bed. The window dribbled with tiny crystals that glistened in the light of the bedside lamp. He put on

99

his pyjamas and switched off the lamp and pressed his face close to the window pane.

The darkness outside was thick with moisture and he could hear the gentle whisper of the rain as it settled on the greenery below. Over towards the valley he could see the misty twinkle of the lights in the village, and he suddenly remembered the men in the bowler hats. He'd forgotten again, to tell Ben. Never mind. He'd tell him in church in the morning or on Monday after school.

He got into bed. Perhaps Ben knew already and thought it was such a daft idea it wasn't worth mentioning. That was probably it. He closed his eyes. Such a daft idea...not worth mentioning at all...

Mr Potter didn't go to the parish church. It was a little on the High side. And he was a Methodist. As his nearest place of worship was in Lotchford, he seldom went to church at all. So he didn't put on his Sunday suit until the afternoon. He generally spent the morning in a leisurely pursuit of odd jobs, mostly in the cottage garden, although the routine changed a bit when Mrs Massiter was away and he and his missus slept at Valley End.

He was usually late to stir on Sundays, and had just returned from the cottage after feeding Bula and collecting milk and papers, when Joe and Mrs Potter were ready for church.

'Having coffee, dear, before you go?' he inquired as his wife entered the kitchen.

'Daniel Potter! Fancy asking! It's hardly five minutes since breakfast!'

Joe pulled at the collar of his new white shirt and looked at the clock and thought what a silly thing it was to say. It took Mrs Potter nearly an hour to get ready for church, and she'd washed up, swept up and made the beds before she'd retired to change. Mind you, she looked very nice when she *was* changed; in the dark tweed skirt and the double-breasted jacket with the lemon blouse underneath just below the amber necklace, and the close-fitting straw bonnet above. She was rather short, and ample at the middle, like Smokey, but then this probably contributed to her good nature.

Although the morning was bright it didn't really look settled, so she borrowed the fawn umbrella and Mr Potter came to the door to see them off.

'You'll bring Smokey in if it rains?' Joe asked him.

Mr Potter said he would, and when they'd gone, he made the coffee for himself and sat down with the Sunday paper.

It was a nice morning for a walk. There was a soft south-westerly breeze tingling with the freshness that comes after rain. Down the valley towards the east, beyond Steeple Green, the sky was deep and wide with a misty lightness paling the blue where it merged with the horizon. Each blade of grass at the roadside sparkled with minute water crystals, and spiders' webs, spun across shallow culverts, glistened silver in the sun. Everywhere the scents of earth, grass and blossom were strong with the drink of rain.

Mrs Potter was a slow walker which gave you plenty of time to admire the view if you were new to the district; but Joe was not very new, and he was anxious to get on and into the village. He was wondering about *The Crown* and the new window and whether he'd meet the landlord. Even if he did know Joe was related to Uncle Bert, he wouldn't say anything in front of Mrs Potter. Joe was sure of that.

They didn't meet the landlord but when they passed the inn Joe could see the new window. He could tell from the fresh strips of putty framing the large pane of glass that things were back to normal in the Tap Room. There was nothing else to show that there'd ever been a scene like the one on Friday night.

So Joe walked on with Mrs Potter, over the green and into church and prayed Uncle Bert would send the compensation.

On Monday morning his prayer was answered in the shape of a parcel from Uncle Bert. It arrived just before he was due to be at the bottom of The Drift for the school bus. When he opened it he found a large box of chocolates with an envelope on top. In the envelope was a long letter and two five-shilling postal orders. Joe put the chocolates in his bedroom with the postal orders, and took the letter to school.

There was too much noise and too many jolts to read it in the bus. Besides, he wanted to read it on his own. But it wasn't until the mid-morning break that he was able to get away from the crowd and have it all to himself.

The letter was dated Saturday and

headed in Uncle Bert's large hand, *S.S Rangitata, Hull.*

Dear Joe, he read, *Larry's not much of a hand with the pen so I'm writing for him as well as myself to apologise to all concerned for the unfortunate incidents on Friday night and Saturday morning. Larry and me sincerely hope that his disgraceful behaviour won't come to Mrs Massiter's ears, for the last thing I would want to do is upset or offend her. As a small token of thanks for so kindly putting us up I'd like you to offer her the box of chocolates I'm enclosing.*

Larry is feeling better now and wants to say how sorry he is to the gent he insulted. As he can't do that 'cause he don't know him (and we're sailing on Monday) he'd be very grateful if you could pass on his feelings, if you can find out what gent it is. The only help I can give you is, he seems to carry cucumber and lettuce around. Larry encloses a five-shilling postal order to cover your expenses, and the other one's from me.

I hope Mrs Massiter found her husband much improved, and I was sorry she had to leave in a hurry as it would have been nice to have had more time for a talk, 'specially as I wanted to tell her about Australia. However, you can tell her what I have in mind. It will be some months yet before we get to the moving stage so you'll have plenty of time to think about coming yourself. I'm sure it'll be the makings of your Aunt Ethel and the baby, but I know it's different for you and Liz.

With Liz having all the looks of getting engaged and you very happy where you are with the late Mr Penny's donkey, you know your aunt and me wouldn't want to influence the choice of either of you. I think Liz is old enough to make up her own mind—you're growing up, too, and you've always seemed to me able to stand on your own feet, so as I told you, you must think it over and of course, talk it over with Mrs Massiter. But, as I says, there's a lot of water to go under the bridge yet.

I'll write you a line from Australia soon as I get an address, and you can tell me how you're going on. Meantime, your Aunt Ethel and the baby'll be pleased to see you any time you can pop over to Brighton.

Your affectionate Uncle Bert

P.S. You'll be pleased to know we've sent the compensation to the landlord.

It was a long letter for Uncle Bert. Joe

folded it carefully and pushed it into his pocket. It brought a nice, warm glow inside, and even the harsh feelings he'd harboured for Larry mellowed a little at the thought of all those kind words, let alone the enclosures. Just like Uncle Bert to smooth down something he didn't even start.

When the call bell rang he went back into class to study the Plantagenet period, but he couldn't concentrate much on history.

As soon as he'd had tea and exercised and stabled Smokey, Joe took the short cut across Prospect Meadow to Ben's place. He found Ben at the fowl run mending the setting hen coop which stood up on legs at the back of one of the huts.

'Gotta coupla setters in there that I want to shut up tonight.' He nodded at the birds in the run as Joe stopped beside him, breathless from his hurried journey.

Ben knocked a new slat into place and gave Joe a closer look.

'You seem a big chuffed, me boy.' He smiled. 'Puffed, too, I reckon.'

'I wanted to tell you I've heard from Uncle Bert.' Joe was feeling in his pocket for the letter and couldn't get words or paper out fast enough. 'It's all right,' he went on, offering the letter to Ben. 'He's sent the compensation. You read it.'

Ben nodded and as he took the letter his smile broadened.

'I know,' he said.

'You *know?*'

'Come, sit yourself down over here.' He moved over to a patch of grass where the remains of an elm stump provided a low seat, and Joe followed with the wheelbarrow, parking himself on one of the shafts.

'How *do* you know?' he insisted.

'I was along wi' Gosling this morning,' Ben said, opening the neatly folded paper. 'He told me he'd heard—apologies and a fiver. So wi' the two he's already got on account, he's more'n satisfied.'

'It's too good to be true. That it's all settled so quickly, I mean.' Joe sighed and thrust his hands into the small pockets of his trousers. He sat quietly after that, happily watching Ben read slowly through the letter. About half-way the old man suddenly paused and chuckled softly to himself, and Joe guessed he'd come to the bit about the cucumber and lettuce. He seemed to be reading some of it twice, but at last he looked up, slowly folding the letter and handing it back.

'Very nice, Joe,' he said quietly, turning a little to follow the flight of a hawk over Marley Wood with a strange, faraway look in his eyes. 'Your Uncle Bert's a right nice fella, I reckon,' he went on in the same tone. 'And Larry's no' so bad neither. Just human, like the rest o' us.'

They sat a little longer while Ben filled and lit his pipe, then they went back to the hen coop and Joe helped with the repairs. It was soon after this that he mentioned the reservoir and told Ben about the chauffeur and the men in the bowler hats.

'Oh ay, I did catch a rumour o' it,' he muttered, after hearing Joe out. 'I don't reckon anything'll come o' it in these parts. Too many rich people to raise their voices.' He straightened up, stretching his back. 'But durn me, don't it fair a rum 'un? Building all them houses, getting all them people down and then wondering if there's enough water to go round. Jobs, too. Soon you won't see the country for people and houses and factories and air bases and them nuclar electric how-d'you-dos. It fair makes you sick,' he grumbled. 'All them officials and planners and inspectors riding around in motor cars and telling us what to do when we been doing it all our lives.' He spat into the grass. 'Don't talk to me about 'em.'

Ben was getting so worked up that Joe didn't talk to him about them, and he was glad when they went indoors and finished up the rice pudding left over from Sunday lunch. Joe left the cottage in the early twilight, hopping and skipping his way back to Valley End, but his buoyant spirits flagged a little when he reached the house and heard the news.

Mrs Potter met him as he crept in at the kitchen door.

'You're late, Joe,' she scolded mildly. 'It's nearly dark.'

'It's all right.' He smiled. 'I was over with Ben. Something special.' He looked at her. 'Have you heard anything from Mrs Massiter?'

Mrs Potter nodded.

'She rang about an hour ago.'

'When is she coming back?'

'Towards the end of the week, she says. Probably Friday or Saturday.' Mrs Potter hesitated as if the final piece of news had caught in her throat. 'Mr Massiter's coming with her.'

Joe was numbed. So surprised he didn't grasp it at first.

'What—to stay?' he said at last.

'Well, o' course. I've got to get the large guest room ready.'

'For how long?'

'Who knows?' Mrs Potter shrugged. 'He's got to have a nice long rest. That's all I can tell you.'

Joe went to bed troubled by the news. How long was a long rest? What changes would Mr Massiter's presence make at Valley End? On the few occasions Joe had seen him he'd noticed a difference in the man. A difference for the better. But popping down for an occasional visit was not quite the same as staying with you for weeks on end. Anything that threatened the happiness he shared with Mrs Massiter was too fearful to think about.

He thrust the thought away from him and tried to be fair to Mr Massiter. After all, the man was ill, and he *had* given Joe a bike and a pair of field glasses. Although he might seem an intruder at Valley End, he was still Mrs Massiter's husband. For all that, Joe couldn't suppress a niggle of fear the thought of his stay aroused.

It was different in the morning. Funny

how the sunshine could douse the fears of the night. He felt a lot better, and this optimism remained with him over the next two days. School and Smokey's training seemed to keep the future at bay. On Wednesday when he called at the cottage, anxious for Ben to know, he was disappointed to find no one there. On Thursday he was worried again, although he did try to look on the bright side. Things might not be so bad. Perhaps Mr Massiter wouldn't stay long. Perhaps even now he'd changed his mind and wouldn't come at all.

But when he got off the bus on Friday the Rolls-Royce was in the drive, and Joe knew that he was there.

CHAPTER 7

Mr Massiter was in bed when Joe arrived. He was tired after the journey though he'd come all the way in his Rolls. Mrs Massiter had sat with him in the back, and one of the company's drivers had followed with her estate car.

The two chauffeurs had tea in the kitchen and went back to London in the Rolls, and soon after they'd gone the doctor called. He didn't stay long, but with all the fuss and the people and the coming and going, Joe and Mrs Massiter never had a chance to manage more than a kiss-me-quick Hallo. In fact, it wasn't until the house had settled down again and the guest was asleep that they were alone for the first time, though they could still hear Mrs Potter clearing the table in the dining-room.

But the lounge was quiet and relaxing. Joe sat down and watched her and didn't know what to say. She hadn't eaten much. He'd noticed that. She looked tired and played out, as if she could do with a long rest herself. Her warm, dark eyes were dulled at the edges where the shadow had washed the sparkles away. Her mouth was a little drawn, but it relaxed when she smiled at Joe.

She pushed a dark curl into place and moved over to the cabinet.

'Would you like a lemonade, Joe?'

'Yes—well—shall I get it?' Joe was about to rise, his eye panicking on the cabinet, but she didn't notice any change in the rum bottle when she opened the door.

'I'll see to it,' she said. 'I think I could do with a drink myself. It's been quite a day.'

She put Joe's glass on the silver tray and poured herself a little brandy and water. She brought the tray to the coffee table and sat down in the deep arm-chair.

Joe glanced hesitantly up at the ceiling. 'How—how—is he?'

'Much better. You'll see him in the morning.'

'Was it very bad?'

'Well, quite serious, though it could have been much worse.' She took a sip from the glass. 'He was near a state of collapse. Overwork. But then, no one could tell Arnold when to stop. He hasn't been looking after himself, neither has there been anyone to look after him. At least, not in the way he needs. I think he'll get on quickly now, down here, provided we can make him forget his precious business. At any event, he's away from it.'

'Is he—will—he be staying long?' Joe coloured a little at his impertinent question. He had no right to ask, and hurried on: 'Well, I mean, say, until the flower show and fair?'

'Oh, I don't know about that—they're in September aren't they?'

'Yes. Second Saturday.'

'I don't know. It depends.' She looked into her glass as if she could see the future there. 'He'll stay just as long as it takes him to get well. Well enough to return to his affairs.' She looked up again, studying the boy who'd filled the gap in her life. 'You know, it won't make any difference to us, Joe; to you, and our life here. At least, we might change the routine a little. When he's ready to get about we ought to show him round. You could do that: introduce him to Smokey; take him for walks. He said he was looking forward to that.'

'He did?' Joe was surprised. 'So—he really wanted to come?'

'Yes, Joe,' she said softly. She looked into the glass again. 'He really wanted to come.'

She sipped at the drink and Joe took a great gulp of lemonade. It was a moment or two before she looked at him again, and when she did the sparkles were coming back once more. She patted the arm of her chair invitingly.

'Come and sit over here,' she said. 'And

tell me how Ben is and all that's happened while I was away.'

Joe went over and told her. But not what had happened at *The Crown*. He stuck to Ben's advice and didn't mention the unpleasant parts. She wanted to know about Uncle Bert and his shipmate and if they'd had a comfortable night, and Joe remembered then to run upstairs and get the box of chocolates. She was very impressed with these and thought Uncle Bert was sweet, but she got rather anxious when Joe told her about Australia. He wished he could show her the letter that referred to all that, but he couldn't cut it in half, and even if he did there were Uncle Bert's apologies on the other side. So he explained the plans, but said he didn't want to go and that his relatives wouldn't try to persuade him. She was still further impressed by this, and said that as soon as Mr Massiter was well she would arrange a car to bring Aunt Ethel and the baby and Liz, too, to Valley End for a few days and they could talk everything over.

She was very interested in the donkey race when Joe went on to explain about Colonel Rawlins, and she said she would ring him up after the week-end. 'I don't think Mr Massiter will want to see any callers for a couple of days,' she declared.

But he saw Joe in the morning, after he'd had breakfast in bed. He came down in light flannel trousers with a silk shirt under his summer smoking jacket, but he hadn't got a cigar. Potter had put out the deck-chairs with their gay sunshades on the lawn, close to the garden hammock, and after he had seen Mr Massiter comfortably settled Joe sat down in an upright canvas chair.

'Well, Joe,' Mr Massiter smiled faintly. 'For the first time in many years I am in a position to appreciate my surroundings. Enforced, mark you, but nevertheless, very welcome. I must make the most of it. And I want you to show me all that I've been missing ever since—well, perhaps ever since I was a boy.'

Joe nodded, and said he would. Somehow he'd never imagined Mr Massiter being a boy. And now he looked almost an old man. He wasn't, of course. It was his illness. Although Joe was surprised to see him looking not all that bad. He was a bit thinner and pale about the gills, and his eyes were sunk a little, but there was nothing feeble about him. A little more grey had replaced the dark hair at his temples, but on top it was still thick and glossy. His manner was softer and his voice warmer, and when he smiled his thanks for something done you could see he really meant it. He didn't look the thoughtless, powerful business man any more—well, not so much like him, anyway. Illness made a difference. It cut you down to size. It let you see you were made the same way as all the other people. It didn't matter if you were successful and confident and independent, and had all the money in the world; when you were ill you needed someone, someone to rely on.

Mr Massiter seemed content to rely on Joe and the Potters and, especially his wife. As the early days went by he began to get his colour back, subdued with a touch of suntan, and his mood grew light and buoyant. His world of business, it seemed, was limited to the columns of the daily papers, and you would never have noticed that business was in his mind. Only once was this apparent; when Mrs Potter brought him out a rug because the breeze was chilly, he told her, rather testily, not to fuss. He'd got his nose in *The Financial Times* on that occasion.

Colonel Rawlins called in that first week—on his hunter. He didn't stay long. But he seemed pleased to see Arnold Massiter there. Joe still went over to Ben's place. When he could. But with school all day, Smokey to train, and Mr Massiter to show around the gardens and the paddock, he didn't have much time, even at the week-end. He told Ben about it. And, of course, he understood. He was a bit surprised at first when he heard Mr Massiter was resting there; but he thought to himself that such a man would have nowhere else to go. He didn't mention this thought; but he said the rest at Valley End might make a difference. Illness did, he told Joe. When he was well he might never be the same again. A change for the better, it could be. It happened to people.

It seemed to be happening to Mr Massiter.

Mrs Massiter seemed a little different, too. She'd told Joe the first night that they might have to change the routine a bit; but he hadn't really expected it to make any difference to her. But it did. Not much, mind you. But he noticed it. She seemed to take more interest in the running of the house. She spent more time in the kitchen, cooking the meals as well as planning them, instead of leaving the stove to Mrs Potter. Of course, Mr Massiter had to be careful about his food; his specialist in London had put him on a diet, and Joe thought that might be why she took over the reins.

She was strict about meal times, and there was dinner at night instead of the light evening meal they used to have. It was as if she expected her husband to miss the close attention of the servants and call bells in his house in Regent's Park; as if she was anxious to show that Valley End could provide a better service.

Joe didn't think she rested often—not like she used to. Not even in the afternoons except occasionally, in the garden, when Mrs Potter brought tea out on the lawn at four o'clock. Of course, Joe wasn't there all day from Monday to Friday, and perhaps he never had time to get used to the changes, so he noticed them more. But they were natural, when you had a guest in the house. And Mr Massiter wasn't any guest. So in the circumstances you'd expect her to be concerned for his welfare. But putting on a pretty summer dress to cut the flowers when she'd nearly

119

always worn slacks in the morning—well, Joe couldn't see how that had much to do with welfare. Still, a woman might do just that, especially when the guest in her house was a man.

She never went out much. She was always on hand. Like a nurse, really. Sometimes she'd get Mrs Potter to report if Mr Massiter required anything. Sometimes she'd ask Joe. But mostly she'd see for herself.

Joe sometimes wondered what illness *he* could have to get the same attention. Of course, it might have been just his fancy. She'd never really changed towards him. So perhaps there wasn't so much difference after all. Still, you *noticed* it.

It was at the end of the third week that Mr Massiter's specialist called. He came down from London in a chauffeur-driven Bentley and stayed to lunch. Joe seldom got home from school before four-thirty so he didn't see the visitor until the man was leaving.

He spotted the car and the chauffeur sitting in the drive, so he went round the back to the kitchen. He was going through to the front when Mrs Potter caught him in the hall, a finger to her lips and her voice hushed up.

'Ssh!' she breathed. 'You'd better go up and wash and change those dirty shoes. The specialist is here.'

'Who?' exclaimed Joe.

'*Sir Vincent Craig.*' It was an awed whisper now. 'He treats the Royal Family.'

'Treats them to what?' Joe still couldn't get the message.

'Ssh! He's a famous doctor, silly. Been here all day.'

Joe looked alarmed. 'He—hasn't collapsed— has he—Mr Massiter?'

'O' course not. They're friends. Just came to see how he was. They're all in the lounge.' She pushed him quietly towards the stairs. 'Go up and tidy. Madam might send for you when she knows you're home.'

'I'm not ill.'

'Go on with you.' She squeezed his arm. 'Quick!'

Joe crept upstairs and into his room. It was when he came out of the bathroom, that he heard them in the hall. He paused on the long, wide landing, leaning his ear over the banister. But he couldn't catch much, only the sound of the latch as they

121

opened the front door.

He slipped into Mrs Massiter's bedroom that overlooked the drive, and peered down on the car through the white mesh curtains. The chauffeur stood to attention with the rear door open, and a white-haired man in a dark grey suit stepped from the porch into view.

He looked quite smart, but there was nothing posh or up-in-the-air about him. In fact, he had a very relaxing manner and a sort of easy-to-talk to face that Joe wouldn't have thought went with titles. His voice was soft, too, though Joe could hear every word through the open window.

'A delightful day, Laura.' He smiled. 'I don't know when I've enjoyed a professional visit more.'

'It's been a pleasure. I hope you'll come again; for the week-end.' That was Mrs Massiter's voice, although Joe couldn't see her or the patient because the roof of the porch blocked them out.

'I don't think Arnold is in need of further medical attendance.' He was still smiling as he held out his hand and Joe could just see Mrs Massiter's slim arm as they shook hands.

'It's the only way to drag Vincent out

of Town—tempt him with a professional engagement.' Mr Massiter was actually chuckling. 'I'll see you in London.'

The specialist waved his finger and the smile almost vanished.

'Not yet, Arnold. Not yet. Unless you want to undo all the good Laura has done for you.' He moved a pace nearer the porch. 'Now you must take my advice, and keep away from the office unless you want us to start at the beginning again.'

'I'm not going to hurry,' Mr Massiter said. 'But there'll be things needing my attention. I'll have Fisher run down.'

'Well, provided there'll be no pressure.' He moved back to the car, and they all stepped into view then. 'But you'll have to leave active business affairs for at least another month.' He shook hands with Mr Massiter and entered the car, leaning out of the open window. The chauffeur touched his cap and slid behind the wheel.

'Remember the tonic,' added Sir Vincent Craig. 'A good walk each day. And you can take him slowly off the diet, Laura.'

Mrs Massiter nodded and waved, and they stood in the drive and watched the car purr away.

Joe hesitated a moment. Just as the two in the drive seemed to be hesitating. Then he saw them turn and look at each other.

Mr Massiter smiled first. He looked so well and amiable Joe was sure he'd had the tonic. He watched them enter the porch and heard a soft gush of laughter, but he couldn't hear what was said. Perhaps Mr Massiter was actually cracking a joke?

Joe went back to his room, and stared at his dirty shoes. It was surprising what a tonic could do.

CHAPTER 8

It was towards the end of July, just after the start of the school holidays, that Joe began to sense which way the wind was blowing.

The clover had been cut, the corn was turning gold and the sky was blue; but a tiny thread of cloud was blowing a trace of shadow across the longest summer days of his life.

He should have been very happy the way

things had turned out, and indeed, he was, so far. Nothing more had been heard of the incident at the inn and the Massiters remained in ignorance of it; he was grateful for that. And the benevolent change in Mr Massiter's attitude, which had grown more pronounced as the weeks went by, should have augured well for the future. But it was just this change that seemed to bring the uneasy feeling niggling at the back of Joe's mind.

It became more apparent during the first long walk on which he and Mr Massiter embarked. Mrs Massiter suggested it the day after the Company's Mr Fisher had been down. And perhaps they could call in at Ben's place on the way, she added. Joe thought perhaps they could do that and, if there was time afterwards, they might go on through the edge of Marley Wood as far as Tyler's Knoll.

So it was settled, and soon as they'd finished breakfast, they set off for Prospect Meadow. Mr Massiter had a walking stick, not so much to lean on as to steady him over the uneven ground. He was used to pavements when he walked at all. But he got on quite well, walking slowly, and pausing now and then to look around, as if he was enjoying it. Joe wondered if he was really totting up the landscape in pounds, shillings and pence. For despite Mr Massiter's change of manner, Joe realised that nothing would change his sense of business, and whenever Joe pointed out the magic of Nature and the contrasting colours that made up the harmony of the countryside, Mr Massiter would just nod his head and look as if he was thinking of something else. Even when they were in the paddock and Joe was showing off Smokey, it was the same. It didn't matter whether they were in the paddock or walking down to Winkletye Lane, his attention was always straying because his mind was somewhere else. Joe thought it was a good sign really: a sign that he was better; a sign that he would be going back to London, pretty soon.

They found Ben slashing down a riot of docks and nettles behind the packing-shed, and he didn't know they were there until Joe whistled his attention.

He straightened up and came over, letting go the slasher and wiping the sweat off his hands on the seat of his breeches. He wore no tie; just the usual khaki shirt with the gold-tipped stud fastening the neck, and a corduroy waistcoat, each pocket bulging with a strange assortment of articles from bits of binder twine and a tin of tacks to a four-bladed penknife and a farmer's diary. Mr Massiter had no bulges at the pockets, and the contrast of fine calf brogues, cavalry twill trousers, silk tie and linen jacket, that graced his person, was very noticeable.

Joe introduced them, and Mr Massiter hesitantly shook hands.

'You'll be right well now, I hope?' Ben said, standing at ease before the impressive visitor, though Joe could see that he wasn't much impressed. He wondered if Ben might address Mr Massiter as *sir*, but he thought that would have been out of character. Ben was too independent to give anyone a title. He feared it smacked of privilege, authority and superiority, and he wouldn't admit nor submit to any of these. Neither, as he put it, would he kow-tow to anyone; it gave the appearance of currying favour. They took him as he was, or not at all.

'I'm very fit, thank you.' Mr Massiter spoke in polite, distant tones with a trace of brusqueness that reminded Joe of earlier days.

You could understand it. He wasn't at home here. He'd never been so close to the earth before, although he'd built on it all over the place.

The silence that followed the brief opening remarks was becoming a bit awkward for Joe, and he had to think of something. After a moment, he thought of the ducks.

'Are the mallards about?' he asked.

Ben glanced towards the pool, shaking his head.

'Haven't seen 'em for some time now,' he said.

'Nor have I,' Joe said. 'I thought they might be at the pond in Marley Wood.'

'Ay, they chop and change a bit,' Ben agreed. 'But I reckon it's more'n likely they're over on the Darren Hall estate, yonder.' He nodded vaguely down the valley.

'Estate?' murmured Mr Massiter. 'I didn't think there were any estates in existence nowadays.'

'Ay, well, it ain't like it was. More's the pity. Been cut up a bit this past fifteen years. But there's a few hundred acres left. Mostly grassland and marsh. It's a game and wild fowl farm now. Our M.P lives there when he's home, but he doesn't have much to do wi' the running o' the place. Gotta manager in the lodge.'

'Of course,' Joe said. 'I'd forgotten about the farm. I expect our ducks spend most of their time around there.'

'You'll be a sporting man, Mister?' Ben inquired.

'Afraid not,' Mr Massiter smiled. 'My companies give me very little opportunity for other pursuits.'

Ben nodded in sympathy.

'Ay, you have to keep at it to earn yourself a living these days,' he said.

They didn't stay long, and Joe was glad when they left. He felt awkward with Mr Massiter there. In fact, he felt awkward with anyone there. When he was with Ben it was never the same when they had company. They got along best alone. It just went to show how they suited each other.

Mr Massiter was a little tired when they reached Tyler's Knoll. They'd turned off the lane at the corner and taken the track by the stream, and Joe led him along the path through the eastern edge of the wood and across the grass field rising gently to the Knoll. It was a long, shallow hummock of land on the slope of the valley, topped by a cluster of birch trees.

Mr Massiter sat down on a birch log, too hot and weary to notice the ants scurrying about their work over the decomposing bark. He mopped his forehead with a handkerchief, irritated by his omission to bring his summer hat. But it was cooler in the sun-speckled shade of the trees, and the view was soothing.

Joe sat cross-legged in the warm-scented grass, and pointed out the landmarks he knew so well. Mr Massiter didn't care for field study rambles, but he was impressed with Joe's knowledge. The boy had never stopped talking since they'd left the cottage, and Mr Massiter's mind was so confused with the facts of Nature, the species of bird and animal haunting the wood, that the monologue was now beginning to go in one ear and out the other. He would have preferred to have just sat and looked for a while, but there was no stopping Joe.

He pointed down the valley to where the stream broadened out. That was where the ducks were, he explained. Darren Hall. You couldn't see the house, but the land went down to the river. Mr Massiter looked, but not for long. His vision wasn't all that good without glasses. So Joe indicated the nearer places. He didn't think Mr Massiter could tell the difference between wheat and barley, so he told him. The fields made a soft pattern of colour across the valley, the deep gold of the wheat, the barley and oats in lighter shades, the green tops of the sugar beet, and the dark dried look of the beans.

Mr Massiter didn't know all the fields had names, so Joe began to point them out ...Larkspur—Black Vine—Sandhill—Beglands—Gawslands—Drippingpan—Highfield ...right along the sweep of the valley to Prospect Meadow...the names dripped from his tongue as if he were reciting poetry.

Mr Massiter nodded thoughtfully. He could see how much Joe knew and liked the country, but that wouldn't add up to much in the commercial world. And that's where Joe's future lay—in the commercial world, where the money was. You could always get back to the country afterwards, if you wished. These past few weeks at Valley End had given him time to think, and he'd been thinking a little about Joe's future. Given the right leads and the backing he was sure the boy could make his mark in the world. Perhaps in the property world. And a good school was the start. He was sure this was what Laura would want if the boy was going to remain under her guardianship. He had really been expecting her to broach the subject, for something would have to be arranged soon. Meanwhile, he thought the moment opportune to introduce the subject to Joe.

He ran the tip of his handkerchief inside his collar to cool his neck, and cleared his throat.

'You seem to have made good use of your time here, Joe,' he smiled. 'There doesn't seem to be much you're not aware of in this part of the country.'

'I like it here.'

'I know. And when you like something you're quick to learn. But you're doing very well at school too, I hear.'

'School isn't bad, but it's not like being out here or in the wood. It's where everything happens. And it's happening all the time.' He looked round at the log, seeing the ants working there, and added, 'Nothing much happens in class.'

'That depends on the school.'

'Don't think any school could show

me what Ben has. He's learnt me all I know.'

Mr Massiter winced.

'The word is *taught*, Joe,' he corrected gently. 'Ben has *taught* you all you know.'

'Yes, I meant *taught*,' Joe said apologetically.

'He may have taught you all you know about the countryside and the animals; but it's far from the world in which you have to make a career.'

Joe looked up at him with a pained expression.

And Mr Massiter hurried on, 'What I mean to say is, the knowledge you've acquired is excellent in itself, and very useful, too, in many ways, but it won't help you much in the keen competitive business world. A very different world from—well, from Pollard's.'

'But there's nothing wrong with Ben's life.'

'Of course not—for people like him. But it's very limited, Joe, in every way, and I think you're capable of wider things.'

'I just want to be like Ben, that's all,' Joe said.

'You'll feel very differently when you grow up. You can take that from me.'

Mr Massiter took a deep breath and suddenly noticed the ants. He moved away. 'Why, this is just a summer holiday, this time you've had down here. And summer holidays only last so long—even at your age. I would not have expected you to think seriously of the future, but someone has to consider it.'

Joe leaned back on his hands and felt the moving grass stir his fingers as the breeze rippled the slender blades. It was a nice feeling. All the magic and the freedom of the wide open spaces seemed symbolised in the moving grass and the gently swaying trees. This was Ben's world; the best of all worlds. Joe didn't want to know any other.

'I've been considering it, Joe, particularly these last few days,' went on Mr Massiter. 'And we have to start off with a good school.'

'School? I'm already going to a good school.'

'Yes, yes. Perhaps so. But you're growing beyond it now. The right school gives you a good basis on which to build. You can't expect to build very high with a poor foundation.'

Joe didn't want to build high. He just

wanted to stay close to the earth.

'One good school I had in mind was Shelbourne. I know the principal there.'

'Where?'

'Shelbourne in Hampshire. You would go on from there to university. Oxford or Cambridge.'

Joe's face clouded over. He didn't know much about Oxford and Cambridge, except that they had a boat race. Of Shelbourne he knew nothing. But he could guess.

'You mean—you have to go away—live there? It's that sort of school?'

'Yes. You'd be a boarder. It's a fine school with a great deal of influence, providing an excellent background.'

Joe didn't care about backgrounds. All he was concerned with was the life he was living now, that such a school would take away. And take him away from Smokey and Ben and Valley End. That was the trouble with Mr Massiter, he couldn't seem to see that anyone could be happy to live the way they wanted to if that meant living without all the trappings of success and money. It had been just the same with Mr Penny. Mr Massiter thought money would make up for losing a way of life that Mr Penny had chosen of his own

135

free will. Mrs Massiter was different. She understood.

'But Mrs Massiter's never said anything about going away to school,' Joe said.

'I'm sure she would have had it in mind, Joe. She would want you to have every possible chance in life.' Mr Massiter lit a cigarette to divert the course of a cloud of midges. 'She probably wants to have a talk with your relatives before discussing it with you. They're going to Australia, aren't they?'

'Yes,' said Joe, dully. 'That's where they're going.'

'Well, Laura must get in touch.' Mr Massiter rose slowly to his feet. 'Time is running out and it may take a little while to get things settled. So we have to make a start very soon.'

They went back a different way, coming out on the main road near the old round house which was all that remained of the once proud post mill. Joe was quiet with thought on the journey. It wasn't surprising when you thought what the thought was, and even when they reached Valley End and Mrs Massiter told them Colonel Rawlins had called, it didn't lighten the load on Joe's mind.

'He stayed for a drink,' she explained. 'And we talked about the flower show; but he really wanted to talk to us both, Arnold.'

'Not about the show?'

'No.' She frowned, her dark eyes anxious. 'He said there's a scheme to build a reservoir in the valley. At least, the valley is one of the sites to be investigated.'

'I heard about it,' Joe said. 'But Ben said it was only a rumour.'

'Obviously, Colonel Rawlins doesn't think so,' she went on. 'He's very concerned about it and so are the parish and district councils. He's forming a committee. They're going to take the matter up with the County Planning Officer and—other bodies, and he wants our support.'

'What did you say to that?' Mr Massiter glanced out of the window, but it wasn't one that overlooked the valley.

'Naturally, my being a resident, he knew he could count on me. But, of course, I couldn't speak for you.'

Mr Massiter nodded.

'I'm not a ratepayer here,' he said. 'I can't see of what use I could be.'

137

'You know several people at the Ministry, Arnold.'

'That's true. But even if they had any influence concerning such a project, what could you expect? They'd probably say if the district needs more water, then someone has to have a reservoir on their doorstep.'

'Colonel Rawlins says the alternative site at Wyanstone is more suitable in every way. They're hoping to put up their own engineers to conduct an independent investigation. Anyway, he's anxious for everyone's support, and wanted to see you. So I suggested he came over to dinner to-morrow.'

Mr Massiter nodded approvingly. 'I'll be delighted to make his further acquaintance,' he said.

Joe didn't eat much lunch. He hadn't much to say at the table either. And no wonder when he had a reservoir on his mind as well as a boarding school. He went out to the stable and collected the saddle on his way to the paddock. But he didn't begin the exercise routine. He slipped the saddle on Smokey, then stood by the paddock gate with his arm around the donkey's neck, gazing across the valley and into the Future.

The reservoir was one thing. But the boarding school was worse, and more personal. If he had to go away to—where-was-it?...Hampshire, he wouldn't see the reservoir if they built one, anyway, except perhaps in the holidays. Still, he wouldn't like to know the valley was filled with water. But he didn't think it would happen. Ben had said it wouldn't. And there were so many people against it that he didn't see how it could. Colonel Rawlins would have everyone on his side. But Joe had no one to help him solve his problem. Even Ben couldn't do that. The only person he could turn to was Mrs Massiter. After all, she was the one. She was responsible for him. She loved him. Just as he loved her. His future was nothing to do with Mr Massiter. It was her choice—and Joe's. He would have to talk to her. Alone.

But for the rest of the day he never had the opportunity. If Mrs Potter wasn't there Mr Massiter was, and if Joe did catch Mrs Massiter alone, the others were too near for him to risk bringing up the subject.

It wasn't until the next afternoon that his chance came. While they were having tea on the lawn. Mr Massiter had to leave them to take a telephone call from London. Calls from the company were always long ones, so as soon as he had gone Joe put his cup on the garden table and leaned forward.

'Has Mr Massiter ever said anything— about me?' he asked softly.

Mrs Massiter leaned back with her elbows on the arms of the garden chair and her hands together, her long delicate fingers intertwined.

'Said anything, Joe? Well—yes, quite frequently.' She was smiling at him, her dark eyes warm and faintly amused. 'He thinks you're a very nice boy. Considerate and intelligent and—'

Joe waved his hand and coloured a little, interrupting gently: 'No, I don't mean that—I mean—about the future. About going—away—to some school—with a good background?'

Mrs Massiter leaned forward a little then, and looked very thoughtful.

'Why—no, I don't think he's ever mentioned it.'

'Well, he mentioned it yesterday. While we were on that long walk. We sat down, up on Tyler's Knoll, and he said he'd been thinking about my future. About some

140

school in—Hampshire—or somewhere like that. But I'd have to go away—leave here—and you and Ben and Smokey.' He got up and went to her, sinking on to the grass, at her feet. 'But you wouldn't want me to leave, would you?'

She put her hand on his head, gently ruffling his hair.

'Of course not, Joe,' she said. 'I hadn't thought about a boarding school. Naturally, I've been thinking about your education; but I hadn't made up my mind about the actual school.' Her hand dropped to his shoulder. 'I wanted to talk to your relatives about it. Particularly now, when they're going to Australia.'

'They're not going yet, so there's heaps of time.'

She looked at him.

'Time goes very quickly and young people grow fast.' She smiled. 'And your future with me hasn't been settled yet—I mean, officially settled.'

'I know that'll be all right.'

'I'm sure it will, but solicitors have to draw up documents and things to make it permanent and legal. Your aunt has been very kind about it all.'

'She's pleased really. That I've got

someone like you. What with her not being too well, and not having much room in Brighton, she thinks I'm very lucky. And so does Liz.'

'I'm the lucky one,' Mrs Massiter said, folding back the crumpled collar of his shirt. 'We must have them come over.' She suddenly put her finger to her lips. 'I know. We'll invite them next month—say about the middle. They must come for a week and I'll have a car collect them.'

'Liz might be at work.'

'Well, if she is, she can come another time or at the week-end. Yes...' Mrs Massiter went on thoughtfully. 'The middle of August would be nice. We'll have the house to ourselves, and we can talk everything over.'

'Won't Mr Massiter be here?'

'No. He's going away on the 15th.'

Joe sat up, his face brightening.

'You mean—he's—leaving—?' He could not complete the question.

'He'll be coming back. It's business in the Bahamas.'

'Ba—what?'

'Bahamas—the West Indian Islands.'

'Oh, yes. We've had them in the geography lesson. It's a long way.'

142

'The sea trip would do him good, but he can't spare the time.' She spoke disapprovingly. 'He's going to fly.'

'How long will he be away then?'

'Just over a fortnight, he thinks. But at least he's going to see Sir Vincent Craig before he leaves, for a final check-up.'

Joe was encouraged. 'Don't suppose he'll have much time to think any more about me—and that school, then, so p'raps we can find something nearer. There must be one just as good in Colchester or Bury and they're not so very far away. So I could come home every day.'

'We'll see, Joe. We'll see. We'll wait until your Aunt Ethel's been down. Then we'll talk about the future.'

Joe got up as he heard Mr Massiter on the terrace.

'And you won't—you won't take notice of *him?*' he pleaded.

She smiled.

'He's really only thinking of you, Joe,' she said softly. 'You know that. We should be grateful for his advice. But don't worry. I don't want you to go away. And we shall talk everything over together before it's settled.'

Joe went back to his chair. It was a

143

great relief. He felt more like eating now. So he ate the remainder of Mrs Potter's chocolate cake.

Colonel Rawlins didn't mention the reservoir over dinner. He talked about the flower show and the gymkhana and the other attractions of the day. He hoped Mrs Massiter was going to put in some entries, and he told Joe the donkey race was on.

'Mr Hawton will be sending you the entry form,' he continued. 'He's the Sports and Entertainments Secretary.'

'Will there be many donkeys in the race?' Joe asked.

'Enough to make it worth while, I think. Up to now, and including you, Mr Hawton is sure of three, but it's early days yet.' He smiled across the table. 'How's the training going?'

Joe said it was going well. Mrs Massiter thought it would be an exciting day and Mr Massiter said he hoped his affairs would allow him to be available at the time. The Colonel hoped so, too, but you could see he preferred Mr Massiter to be available for more important things. He was really waiting for a lead, which eventually came from Mrs Massiter, just before they withdrew for coffee in the lounge.

'I haven't seen anything in the local Press about the reservoir scheme, Colonel,' she said. 'I can't think that such a plan would materialise with all there is at stake in the valley. People's homes, farms and good agricultural land, as well as the beauty of the valley itself.'

'Unfortunately it's a most likely event if early and very strong objection is not made by all concerned,' Colonel Rawlins declared firmly. 'The Waterboard Authority consider that natural supplies will be insufficient to meet the needs of development in this area after the next five years, and artificial resources will be necessary. At the moment the Authority, with the approval of the Ministry, are considering two possible sites—the valley here, and another farther down, near Wyanstone.'

'How much land is needed?' Mr Massier inquired.

'Between four and five hundred acres is the estimate.'

Joe thought that was a lot of acres. But he didn't say anything. He just went on listening carefully, expecting Mrs Potter to interrupt the proceedings at any moment with the coffee.

'Does the Wyanstone site provide that area?' Mrs Massiter asked.

'More than enough,' the Colonel nodded.

'But I suppose local objections to the scheme there are just as prolific and authentic as they are here?' Mr Massiter suggested.

'No. The conditions are very different. You see, for one thing, the area is sparsely populated. Secondly, the land itself is not as rich. Much of it is not under arable cultivation, and some of it is not cultivated at all.'

Mr Massiter looked mildly surprised. 'Then what is the Authority's objection to making a decision in favour of the site there?'

'Just a minor technical problem, which really isn't a problem at all. It means that the damming of the stream—which broadens somewhat there—would need to be a little more extensive than would be the case here. There would also be a certain amount of excavation. In other words, it means a little more money.'

'Ah.' Mr Massiter gave a wry little smile. He knew all about money, and

Joe wondered what he would have said if Mrs Potter hadn't announced at that moment that she had served coffee in the lounge.

Joe followed them through and while Mrs Massiter dealt with the Cona, her husband poured the brandy and offered their guest cigars. Joe didn't like black coffee so he had it well milked down and although the time was getting on he didn't get a bed-time signal. He parked himself alongside the Sheraton table with its huge bowl of roses as he seemed more unobtrusive there, and watched Colonel Rawlins illustrating his talking points with the aid of sketch maps of the sites.

Joe was really too far away to catch all that was said, but it seemed the Colonel was inviting Mr and Mrs Massiter to join the Valley Protection Committee which he himself was at present organising and which would have the full support of all residents in the area as well as the councils and the Planning Officer.

Joe finished his coffee at this point and took the cup slowly to the trolley. He could hear better there.

'I'm going to arrange a small dinner party where the principals can talk it over with our M.P,' Colonel Rawlins went on. 'I should be very happy if you and Mrs Massiter could come along.'

'We'll be delighted,' Mrs Massiter said. 'Commander Lawson and his wife should be there, and the doctor, the vicar—possibly Mrs Chester-Smyth, and two or three other proposed members of the committee. And I'll arrange it as soon as I have some idea when Philip Luxton is available. He's abroad just at the moment, and I don't suppose he'll be at Darren Hall until the summer recess.'

'At least he's an M.P with a residence in his constituency.' Mrs Massiter smiled. 'He'll be personally concerned with the problem.'

'Quite so.' The Colonel nodded. 'I think we can count on him to play a leading part.'

Mr Massiter sipped slowly at his brandy.

'Of course, my interests are mainly concentrated in London,' he said at length. 'And I'm not expecting to be here very much during the next few weeks; but if you're prepared to suffer a frequently absent committee member, I'll be pleased to give you all the support I can.'

Colonel Rawlins seemed very happy with

this, and so was Joe, although he realised he was making himself more noticeable by hanging around the coffee trolley. He started to make for his chair, but hadn't gone two paces when Mrs Massiter's voice pulled him up and around.

'It's getting late, Joe,' she said. 'I think you'd better say good night.'

He nodded and went back, pausing beside her. She raised her eyes and he felt the warmth and security of all her affection glowing there.

He bent and kissed her and said good night, and went slowly up to his room. But he couldn't sleep. His mind was filled with reservoirs, protection committees and maps as well as pumping stations and filter plants. He was sure everything was going to be all right now, just as Ben had said, but he still couldn't sleep. Even when he heard Colonel Rawlins drive away it didn't make any difference. He lay there, wriggling his toes and saying his prayers, his eyes shut but wide awake. He heard movements on the stairs, doors open and close. Then the soft patter of rain on the window. And that was the moment he heard Smokey. The high and low notes of his braying voice came through Joe's window from the direction of the paddock... He hadn't brought the donkey in!

He leaped out of bed and into his dressing-gown, angrily chiding himself. So intent had he been to hear all Colonel Rawlins had to say that he had gone into the lounge to listen instead of bringing Smokey in from the paddock. To think he'd actually forgotten! Never had he done so before.

He grabbed his pocket torch and opened the door. The landing light was burning, and so was the standard down in the hall. Mrs Massiter always left a lamp on in the hall. She didn't care to have the house in darkness all night.

Her bedroom door was closed as Joe crept to the stairs, and he could hear Mr Massiter humming in the bathroom as he tiptoed by. He went quickly down, avoiding the creaks in the treads, and out to the lobby at the back. Stuffing the bottoms of his pyjamas into his wellingtons and slipping on a mac, he unlocked the lobby door and stepped into the garden.

Luckily, the shower was very light, but Mrs Massiter would have made no end of fuss if she knew he was out in the rain in his pyjamas. So he had no intention of giving his movements away.

He found Smokey nudging the paddock gate, his tail between his legs. He seemed very pleased to see Joe and began waggling his ears as soon as the boy spoke. They took the grass path to the stable, avoiding any noise, and ten minutes later a dry and contented donkey had his muzzle in the manger, and Joe was back in the house.

He paused in the hall, looking up at the darkened landing. The standard lamp was softly shaded, and although it lit the stairs, the shadows were deep beyond the banisters above.

Joe climbed the flight carefully. At the top he paused, startled. A soft murmur of voices issued from Mrs Massiter's room, and he could see long slivers of light where the door edged away from the jamb. He stood there wondering for what seemed a long time but it was really only seconds before he moved. As he tiptoed past the door, the light went out. And suddenly, the landing was a dark and lonely place.

He crept into his own room and the voices seemed to follow him there. He hung his dressing-gown on the door peg and sat down on the bed to think. It was nothing to do with him, of course. And yet...in the end, he knew it would be.

He could see which way the wind was blowing now.

CHAPTER 9

Aunt Ethel couldn't come in the middle of August. The baby had whooping cough. But Liz managed it. She was changing jobs in Brighton and had a week to spare. She brought a long letter from Aunt Ethel for Mrs Massiter and a short one for Joe.

It was a good time to come. August. If you liked it hot. Almost as good as the Bahamas. The sky was arched and clear except for an occasional streak of vapour trailing from some high-flying aircraft. The country shimmered in a blue haze pricked here and there by brilliant sparkles where glass returned the glare of the sun. The air was so still that the dust from the combines as they cut and threshed the corn hung over the fields in small, light clouds and gave the drivers dusky faces and red-rimmed eyes.

Ben was out on the stubble helping to cart the straw bales that the combines dropped behind them as they crawled to and fro over the rise and fall of the land. Like the regular farm workers, he had little time to spare through the daylight hours, and when he wasn't in the fields you would find him in Brierley's barn helping to store the grain in the huge metal silos.

It was fine harvest weather. Fine holiday weather, too. It brought the car people out of the towns and you could see them with picnic spreads in field gateways, eating hard-boiled eggs and tinned fruit and fighting away the wasps.

So it was a pity about Aunt Ethel really. The change would have done her good, but in one way Joe was glad she couldn't come. It meant postponing that talk about the future which would lead to the new school. But nothing more had been said about that. For one thing, Mr Massiter had been away in London a lot and when he had been at Valley End he'd been too preoccupied with his own affairs and his trip to the Bahamas to mention the subject to Joe again.

Mrs Massiter hadn't said anything about a new school either. But soon after her husband flew off from London she told Joe about their reconciliation. She didn't know he knew and he didn't say he'd noticed anything. But, of course, quite apart from what he'd seen that night after Colonel Rawlins came to dinner, he could read the message in their manner, see it in their expressions. The whole atmosphere had changed; you could see the barriers were down. And remembering the looks they'd exchanged the day the specialist came, Joe thought the barriers must have started crumbling then.

'We're going to give our marriage a second chance, Joe,' she told him the morning the cable came reporting Mr Massiter's safe arrival in Nassau. 'Not everyone gets a second chance in life. When you do you must be quick to recognise it—or it has gone for good. Anything that may stand in the way—your pride, memories, every feeling turned hard inside you—must be swept aside. It isn't easy. But it's something worth while. Arnold wants to make the attempt. And so do I. So we're going to try again. From the beginning.'

The illness had changed Mr Massiter, but Joe never thought it would change her. Of course, it was really this change in him that had brought about her decision. She hadn't really changed at all because she'd always been generous and forgiving, kind and affectionate. Joe knew that.

'I'm glad you're happy,' he said simply.

She put her arm around him, sensing his concern, knowing there was a spark of jealousy in it.

'Joe,' she said softly, 'it won't make any difference. You know it won't make any difference to you—to us.'

He nodded, and gently broke away, murmuring some excuse about Smokey's training. And he ran to the paddock. Now that she had told him herself it was a fact and no longer an assumption on his part. They'd made it up. And she was happy. Happier than she'd been—perhaps, ever before. He knew he should have been happy for her. After everything she'd given him, too. Was his only gratitude to begrudge her a second chance? He was only thinking of himself, and he should have been ashamed; but he couldn't help it. He knew things would be different; but it was what she wanted. So what could you do?

Liz's arrival softened his feelings a bit and as the days went by the unhappy thoughts Mrs Massiter's admission had provoked gradually melted away. Mr Massiter's absence might have had something to do with it; but Joe began to feel that the days ahead were what you made of them not what you thought they'd be. And with the show and the race and the fair coming up, it was no time to be gloomy about the future.

Liz got on well with Mrs Massiter; but she didn't like the country much. It was a bit too quiet, after Brighton. And she missed Ron. But she talked about him so much it was just as if he was there. She flashed her engagement ring as well as her smile every time she mentioned his name, but she didn't go into detail about what he did. Although she was rather young to be thinking of marriage, Mrs Massiter hoped she'd be very happy.

She spent a lot of time in the garden in shorts and sun-top and looked very pretty with her slim figure, tan and fluffy fair hair. So much so that Mr Potter always seemed to find more weeds to pick whenever she was in the hammock.

She thought Smokey was a pet, and the scenery very nice, but she wasn't keen on walking too far. She did go with Joe to the harvest field when the men were having their morning break, and he introduced her to Ben. But she didn't want to stay because the dust got in her hair, so Joe took her on to the stockyards to see the pigs. She turned up her nose a bit; she wasn't used to the smell and seemed anxious to get back to the hammock. Although she didn't go much for animals, she thought Ben was really cute.

In a way Joe was rather relieved when the week was up and he and Mrs Massiter took her to Colchester station, though he was very fond of her all the same. Mrs Massiter bought her a couple of magazines to read on the train, and gave her a gift token to buy a premium bond for the baby. Mrs Massiter said she'd be writing to Aunt Ethel, and perhaps they could arrange a visit before the summer was over. After all that, the train was due to leave, and Liz leaned out of the window and showered them with thanks.

'I've had a wonderful time,' she said. 'I'll tell Aunt Ethel all about it. I know she'd love to come before the summer's out.'

And they stood on the platform and waved her out of sight.

For the rest of the month routine was

back to normal, and Joe was able to concentrate on Smokey's training. The posters started going up announcing the show and fair. You could see them pinned to tree trunks and farm buildings alongside the road as well as hanging on gateways and in the windows of *The Crown*.

Colonel Rawlins had been over a couple of times to see Mrs Massiter. He'd organised his committee and had arranged the dinner date for late September; it was the only time Philip Luxton could guarantee. The local press was backing the campaign and there were articles and pictures about the reservoir scheme. But nothing had yet been settled and the final decision was still a long way off. Mr Massiter had gone on to Jamaica and didn't expect to be back until the second week in September.

Harvest was going on apace and if the weather held Ben reckoned Brierley's would finish a week before the flower show. Despite the full-time occupation of the harvest days Ben still found time to advise Joe on the final course of training. He'd come up with the special rations, the extra hard food that would give Smokey stamina. He'd got the beans, corn and the chaff from Brierley's. Joe didn't know where he'd got the bran mash from; but he accepted it without question. He took careful note of amounts and times and only fed Smokey at the end of each exercise.

The days slipped by taking the summer with them and the week of the flower show alternated with sunshine and showers, although by Thursday, when the marquees went up, the weather seemed settled again.

Mr Massiter was coming back on the Saturday, regretting he wouldn't be in time for the show. But Mrs Massiter planned to be there; she was putting three entires in the flower classes. She considered her choice carefully, and finally decided on a vase of dahlias, six cut roses and a wicker basket decoration of flowers and foliage. Mrs Potter was entering, too, but in the Miscellaneous Section, with a Victoria sandwich and a honey cake.

Joe wasn't very interested in the exhibits. He had all he could do training Smokey, but he did ask Ben if he was putting anything in the fruit and vegetable classes. Ben said he hadn't the time, he'd got so much of his own work to do which had been neglected through harvest that he didn't think he'd get to the show at all. But, of course, he would try and manage it if only to see Joe and Smokey in the ring.

It was towards the end of that week—Friday, in fact, that Joe met Nina.

As usual, Smokey's first exercise of the day had been early, and Joe had brought him in for his special diet. While the donkey had his breakfast in the stable Joe nipped over to the showground on his bike. He'd got his race entry form for Mr Hawton, and he wanted to see just what was going on, for the view from the paddock of crowded Spring Meadows was too much for him to resist.

He found Mr Hawton staking out the ring, and asked him what the obstacle race entailed. But Mr Hawton smiled and told Joe to wait and see, though he didn't mind describing the other attractions. He'd got a motor cycle display team from the army with a cast of trick riders and, just in case it rained, he'd booked The Sultan and his Fire Eaters.

Joe thought they would be good but he was a little bit puzzled.

'Wouldn't the rain put out the fire before they could eat it?' he asked.

Mr Hawton's smile broadened as if he had been waiting for the question.

'No,' he said. 'If it rains they can give their turn in the tent, but the ground might get too soggy for the motor cyclists to give a display at all. If so we can be sure of at least one attraction after the gymkhana. That is, if it rains.' He stopped smiling and glanced up at the sky. 'But I don't think it will. The forecast is good. Still, you can't always rely on them. You've got to be prepared.'

Joe agreed you had, and went off to prepare himself by taking a look at the pitch he'd been given for the donkey rides. It was on the fringe of the meadow away from the hedge running as far as the show tents. It wasn't far from the other side-shows, but far enough from all the noisy distractions that might frighten Smokey. As it was, Joe wondered about the motor bikes, but summing up the distance he reckoned they wouldn't sound so bad from his pitch.

Over beyond the ring, at the top end of the meadow, the fair was beginning to arrive. Huge pantechnicons of equipment with trailers and caravans were moving into position in a great semi-circle rather like a covered wagon train you see in western films just before an Indian attack. Already some of the generators and living vans had been sited and thick and thin cables were forming dark snakes over the flattened grass. The lorries piled high with the roundabout equipment were shunting about in the centre, their dark sides brightened with gold lettering announcing *Farrow's Travelling Fair*. Quite a few of the amusements had arrived, but Joe couldn't see the Dodg'ems or the Chimps' Tea Party. But there was plenty of time. It was only Friday morning, and the fair didn't open until Saturday night.

Joe rode right round the showground on his bike, noting the layout of everything. As he passed by the ring Mr Hawton waved, and so did his small son Jeremy, who had now appeared to help thread the rope through the loops of the stakes marking the ring. Everyone was busy, and although some were sweating a bit, they looked as bright and gay as the small coloured flags fluttering from the pole-tops of the two marquees.

After lunch Joe saddled Smokey and took him back into the paddock for his second round of exercise. The afternoon was hot, but under the trees on the farther side the grass was still damp with morning dew, and the ground was soft near the ditches from the rain two nights before.

Joe spent half an hour in the saddle then let Smokey roam, while he leaned against the paddock gate dreamily gazing across the valley to Spring Meadows.

From a huddle of vehicles the fair seemed to be taking shape before his eyes. The big roundabout, forming the centre piece, was almost up, just needing the top and the flags to complete it. Another great lorry and trailer crawled into his view and he reckoned it was the Dodg'ems arriving. The distant scene appeared such a hive of industry it suddenly brought home to Joe that he still had much to do, and was dreaming the time away instead of completing his duties. He had all the harness to clean and the saddle to polish, and he'd already allowed Smokey to crop the grass too long.

They went back to the stable and Joe brushed Smokey down, and got out the polish and dusters. He took the three-legged stool and placed it outside the door and sat in the sun with the harness.

And that was the moment he saw the girl.

He heard the footsteps on the fine loose stones that edged the drive, and caught a glimpse of her small, slim figure between two hydrangea shrubs as she stood, hesitant, looking towards the back of the house. She had long black hair and looked nice and cool in a simple primrose dress, but the thing that puzzled him was the watering can. He stood up to get a better view. He hadn't made a mistake. It *was* a watering can. A large green one, made of plastic. She was carrying it in her right hand, and every now and then she swung it slightly, so he knew it was empty.

He put down the harness, stuffed one end of the duster in his pocket and marched across the grass to the drive.

She didn't hear his approach until his shoes crunched the stones. She turned, startled for a moment, then small, even teeth flashed in a smile.

'Hallo,' she said coolly.

Her welcome smile, confident manner and easy *Hallo*, took the wind out of his sails a bit. He was going to ask her what she wanted; instead, he said, 'Can I help you?'

164

'Yes, please.' She held up her can. 'I'd like some water. I tried the cottage first, but there was no reply.' She had a pale oval face and long dark eyelashes. Her eyes were nice, too; large and round, with a touch of the sky in them.

Joe looked at the can, which was bright and clean.

'What—you camping round here then, and run out of water?'

'Well, we haven't got there yet, but it's sort of camping really.'

'What I mean is,' Joe said, trying to get to the point, 'd'you want the water for drinking?'

'Oh, no. It's for the radiator.'

'What—the car radiator?'

'No. Land-Rover.'

Joe took the can. 'Same thing, so the standpipe'll do. It's over by the garage.' And he started to walk towards it, the girl following.

'Daddy's stuck in a hole and the radiator's boiled dry,' she explained.

'Oh—dear, that's bad luck.'

'It often happens.'

'Does it?'

'Getting stuck in places. It's the weight, you see.'

165

'It's pretty heavy then?' He led the way across the concrete apron in front of the double garage.

'Fairly. There're two to pull.'

'Two?' Joe held the can under the tap and splashed the water in. He didn't know what she was talking about. He'd never had much to do with girls of his own age, and this one looked a bit younger than him. He'd thought they were all chatter and giggles; but he hadn't expected them to talk in riddles all the time. But this one looked a bit different somehow, and he didn't want to show his ignorance, so he tried another line.

'Whereabouts are they?' he asked.

'Just along the road.'

'Will you be able to get out all right?'

'Out?'

'Out the hole.' Joe turned off the tap. 'Your father—I mean, will he want any help?'

'Oh, no, thanks.' She shook her head and her hair stirred round her shoulders like dark corn. 'We can manage. It's just the radiator. It leaks a bit.'

Joe felt relieved. He wanted to get back to his own job.

'It's very nice here.' She stood looking

166

round while Joe stood holding the can. 'You're lucky to live in such a lovely place.'

'I like it,' Joe said. He began to walk back into the drive. She leaned towards him.

'I'll take the can,' she said.

'It's all right, I'll carry it down to the road.'

'No, really. I'm very strong.'

Joe stopped. He didn't know what to do. He wanted to be rid of the girl and get back to his cleaning, but he didn't want to seem rude and selfish.

'Your handkerchief's falling out,' she said, and took the handle of the can.

'It's a duster,' he said.

'You were cleaning something?' She glanced round.

They were both holding the can now.

'Harness,' Joe said.

The blue eyes seemed larger. 'Where's your horse then?'

'Haven't got a horse. He's a donkey.'

'Oh—lovely! Where is he?'

Joe nodded towards the stable.

'Can I see?' she pleaded.

'Well—yes, but—what about your father?'

'It won't take a minute.' She let go her

167

side of the handle and Joe almost dropped the can. He lowered it to the ground and they cut across the grass to the stable.

When Joe opened the lower half of the door Smokey had his head against it, just as if he'd been listening to their conversation. The girl began to fuss him, running her fingers between his ears and then putting her arm around his neck.

'He's so cuddly,' she said. 'What's his name?'

'Smokey.'

She repeated the name, making purring sounds close to the donkey's ear.

Joe grinned. He felt very proud. But he was a little bit worried, too.

'Don't want to get him too excited,' he cautioned. 'He's got a big day to-morrow.'

'Has he?' She was looking at Joe, her arm still around Smokey's neck. 'What's on then?'

'Races.'

'I didn't know they had donkey races,' she said.

'Don't think they do usually; but this is special. We're in the gymkhana at the flower show on Spring Meadows.'

Her arm slipped away from Smokey and she stared at Joe.

168

'Spring Meadows? That's where we're going. To join the fair.'

'You are?' Joe was very surprised but wondered why he hadn't cottoned on before. When she mentioned the Land-Rover and the weight and said there were two, he should have guessed she referred to caravans or trailers. And where else would *they* be going but to the fair? 'What d'you do there?'

'We've got the Chimps,' she said.

'Chimps? You mean—it's the Chimps' Tea Party?'

'That's one of the acts. They ride bicycles, too.'

'Well— fancy—!' Joe didn't know what to say, and before he could think of anything, a distant voice came reeling through the stillness from the road...

'Nina...NINA...'

The girl jerked to attention. 'That's me. Mummy calling.' She smiled. 'I'd better go.' She stepped outside and paused, looking at him. 'Who are *you?*'

'I'm Joe.'

She held out her hand, and he took it shyly in his own.

'Pleased to meet you, Joe,' she said. 'Hope you and Smokey win to-morrow—

169

and thanks for your help.' She ran off across the grass to the drive.

Joe stood for a moment, a little bit dazed by the suddenness of it all. Then he closed the stable door and ran after her. He couldn't let her carry the can now. Besides, he wanted to see the Chimps.

They met Nina's mother at the bottom of The Drift. She had the same black hair as Nina, the same blue eyes; just like her daughter really, but of course, bigger all round. She wore dark blue slacks and a white shirt with a bluish scarf folded in the open neck. She seemed pleased to meet Joe when Nina introduced them, and they all hurried along to the top of Winkletye Lane. That's where the hole was.

It was some way from Valley End, but when they got there Joe could see that Nina had overdone it a bit. It wasn't a hole really. Just a long, deep rut in the soft earth at the side of the road near the bend, right opposite the entrance to Winkletye Lane. Still, it was bad enough. The two caravans, with telescopic tent poles and broad lengths of timber on special roof racks, were leaning towards the hedge, their nearside wheels sunk almost to the axles.

Considering the awkward state of affairs, everyone was in a good mood. Even Nina's father when he emerged from the gap between the two caravans having uncoupled one from the other. His hands were grimy and there were oily smudges on his short-sleeved shirt, but his face was clean and broad, and there were dimples in it when he smiled.

'This is Joe,' Nina introduced them. 'He lives in the big house back there, and he got the water.'

'Then he's my boy.' The man beamed down as he took the can. 'More precious than gold, water is, when your supplies are exhausted.' He started towards the gaping bonnet of the Land-Rover. 'You shall have your reward, Joe.'

Joe had to smile.

'Daddy's never serious,' Nina said, a little pompously.

'How could he be, darling, with the family he's got?' Her mother was smiling, too, as she followed her husband.

Joe was looking at the second caravan which was smaller than the first. There was no blatant announcement picked out in gold leaf on the side like so many other vehicles in the fair. Only a small line of

171

letters low down in the righthand corner reading: *Leo & Lavinia Steed's Famous Chimpanzees.* High up, under the edge of the roof, was a wide grille formed by three metal bars. And as he looked, a hairy hand gripped one of the bars and a face appeared behind them.

Nina saw Joe looking and smiled. 'That's Basil.'

Basil immediately started to bob up and down. He kept pulling faces and curling his lips, and seemed to be muttering all kinds of exciting things.

'How many more besides him?' Joe asked.

'Just two. Trudy and the little one, Effie. They're a family, you see.'

'I'd like to meet them.'

'You will to-morrow. Daddy keeps the key. He wouldn't let them out now. They'd only get in the way. And Basil can be naughty sometimes.' She looked at him. 'But you're coming to the fair, Joe?'

'Try to stop me!' He nodded. 'Monday and Tuesday as well.' He moved round to the back to get a view of the other side, stepping carefully to avoid the muddy racks churned by the nearside wheels. There was a similar grille in the wall of the van and a hairy face behind it.

'That looks like Basil again,' he said.

'No, it's Trudy.' Nina stood beside him, laughing softly.

Joe was mystified. 'They look the same to me.'

'I expect they do, but you'll see the difference when you see them all together.'

They stepped back on to the road.

'It's their own special caravan, I s'ppose?' Joe asked.

'Yes. We live in the other one. Well, I only live in it holidays when I'm home from school.'

Joe was going to ask another question, but the engine of the Land-Rover suddenly whirred into life and Nina's father appeared and asked them to add their weight to his as he wedged his shoulder against the rear of the first van. His wife was at the controls, and as the four-wheel drive took up the load they pushed and shoved. Almost at once there was a soft, squelching sound and the vehicles moved forward and on to the road, leaving the Chimps' caravan still leaning in the mud.

It was only a matter of moments to uncouple the first caravan, and reverse the Rover back and hitch on to the second.

And the same routine quickly had it free. A little more shunting and coupling up, and the Steeds were ready to continue.

Leo Steed came back and surveyed the battleground.

'Ah, well,' he said. 'It'll be a warning to others.'

'The ditch is blocked, that's the trouble,' Joe pointed out. 'The water's soaked through the bank and made it boggy underneath.'

'I can see now,' he nodded. 'But it looked firm enough when I pulled over to let the tanker go by.'

'The lorry driver should have been the one to stop,' Nina said, as her mother came up and joined them.

'He *did* take the bend too fast, Leo,' Mrs Steed declared. 'We might have had a head-on collision.'

'No, no, dear. There was room to spare,' he said. 'I was too cautious.' He grinned at Joe. 'And where does it get you? Look at the mess I'm in!' He was indicating his shirt and the muddy stains on his light cavalry twill trousers. 'Is there such a thing as a cleaners in Elmbridge, Joe?'

Joe said there wasn't.

'That's the trouble. Nothing is ever

where you want it.' The grin spread all over his face. 'But what would life be like without troubles? Monotonous, eh?'

Joe thought he was joking, so he just grinned back. They were such a gay family. It must have been the chimps. Animals again, you see. They made all the difference to humans.

Joe followed them up to the front.

'You know the way?' he asked, as they climbed into the Land-Rover.

'Just the other side of Elmbridge, isn't it?' Leo Steed spoke through the open window, his hands on the wheel.

'That's it. First turning on the right from here. Through the village, and the showground's just up the hill on the left. You can't miss it.'

Steed nodded.

'We'll be seeing you there, I hope,' he said. 'And remember, Joe, you've got free entry to our little show any time you wish.'

Lavinia Steed was smiling and said she'd second that. And just when they were going to move off, Nina suddenly leaned right across the steering-wheel and pushed her arm out of the window, her fist closed tight. Joe had to hold out his hand, and she dropped a tiny, black object into it.

'For you and Smokey,' she said. 'And to-morrow. My lucky charm.'

They drove away then, and Joe stood, a little dazed but very happy, in the middle of the road, watching them go.

CHAPTER 10

Mrs Massiter didn't get up on Saturday morning. She wasn't feeling too well. She wouldn't have any breakfast—only a cup of tea. Mrs Potter took it up and told her not to worry about the show exhibits. Mr Potter could take them over in the car, and she would set them out in the tent herself before she put her honey cake and sandwich on display.

The flower decorations had been arranged the night before, so everything was ready when the car was brought to the door. Joe helped to stow the wicker basket on the flat floor at the back, and when Mrs Potter was in the passenger seat, he handed her the vases. With her cake and Victoria sandwich on the floor between her feet, she sat there with the flowers, as solemn as a mourner, while Mr Potter drove gingerly down the drive.

Judging of exhibits began at eleven o'clock so the Potters went off early, but Joe had plenty of time. Colonel Rawlins had telephoned to say Joe could have his horse-box to take his donkey to the ground, and the groom would come up with it at twelve. It was a very good arrangement for not only did it save a long walk, but by the time Joe went the Potters would be back and Mrs Massiter wouldn't have to be left on her own.

Joe went up to see if there was anything he could do, but she said there was nothing she wanted.

'Go on back to Smokey.' She smiled. 'I shall be all right. I'm sure you still have much to do yourself.' She squeezed his hand. 'I'm bitterly disappointed I won't be there to see you ride, Joe, but I wish you all the luck in the world. Take care.'

Joe had everything done by the time the Potters returned, and Smokey waited, fed and saddled in the stable. He had clipped Nina's lucky charm to a ring on the harness, but it wasn't much of an emblem to see. It was a crude image

177

of a cat made of something like black ivory, no larger than a sixpence, and only when you got right up close would you see what it was. He reckoned Nina had found it in a bon-bon or in some Lucky Dip, and although he was as fond of cats as he was of every other animal, he wasn't very keen on this image. He didn't have much faith in it either, and he wouldn't have displayed it on the harness if Nina hadn't given it. Wherever she'd got it she must think a lot of it, and she'd given it to him. After all, if it wasn't much good, it was the thought that counted. That was the main thing. So the least he could do was to show his appreciation. And Smokey didn't seem to mind.

By the time he'd changed into the rig-out Mrs Massiter had bought him, the groom drove up with the horse-box, and Joe went out feeling very professional in his clothes. The jodhpurs were a bit tight, but the boots were neat and cosy and so was the coloured shirt. In the plain, dark jockey cap he looked a bit like a rowing cox.

The groom turned the car and trailer round on the garage apron, and after some hesitation Smokey went up the ramp; and

Joe rode with him in the box in case he got nervous.

It was a lovely day for a show. The flags above the marquees and on the roundabout at the fair, stirred lazily in the light breeze. The sky was a bit hazy in the distance but it didn't look like rain. The sun was warm and the grass was drying, but in the shade of the hedge alongside Joe's pitch the blackberries were damp, the drooping sprays of fruit still moist and glistening with the morning dew.

The groom parked the trailer at the head of the pitch and said he'd be back to take them home at the end of the show. And Joe settled down to set up his base for the afternoon. Mr Hawton had left him a packet of sandwiches and a bottle of Coke with a pail for watering Smokey, and Joe parked himself on the horse-box ramp and ate his lunch.

There were quite a few people already on the ground, most of them officials. P.C Fowler was on the main gate, with a special in the road to direct the traffic, while an inspector and a sergeant were talking with Colonel Rawlins outside the secretary's tent. The A.A man was in the car park, and the ice cream vendor had

179

just arrived, and was shunting his travelling parlour next to the refreshment buffet.

On the other side of the ring stood a table with a microphone, and close to a pole with a cluster of loudspeakers the electrical service van was parked. Beyond the main car park the competitors' enclosure was filling up with cars and horse-boxes, and milling with youngsters, ponies, and mothers and fathers attempting last words of advice. Away from the vibrant scene, the fair at the top of the meadow stood quiet and still, like a painted picture. Not until the twilight came and closed the show would the picture come to life.

But life was now spilling from the gate into the showground, and the pace about the ring was warming up. To the accompaniment of crackling announcements from loudspeakers, stewards dashed to and fro as donkeys and their jockeys collected in the roped-off enclosure near the winning post, for the donkey races were opening the programme.

Despite Nina's lucky charm it wasn't Joe's lucky day. Whether it was the shouting crowds that affected Smokey, or the crackle of the loudspeakers or just the excitement of the scene, Joe didn't know;

but when the racing began Smokey seemed to have forgotten all his training. There were only three races and only six donkeys and each rider a boy, but Joe never made the first three.

He was fourth in the first race because Smokey was cold to start, and in the second he bumped another rider and came a cropper on the turf; and in the third and final event where the course was strewn with obstacles, he lost Smokey altogether. It was so disappointing because he was leading the field and would have undoubtedly won the race if a spectator hadn't collapsed just when Joe was struggling with the last obstacle on the course. This was a long net pegged closely to the ground, and while Smokey stood patiently to one side Joe dived flat and began the long wriggle. He was half-way through when the spectator collapsed in a canvas chair on the roof of his ringside car. The loud report as the chair gave way and thudded on the coachwork, was like an electric shock for Smokey, and he bolted down the course. By the time Joe had struggled out of the net his mount was at the winning post. And Joe walked miserably after him to the sighs and hand-claps of the crowd while all the other jockeys romped home.

It was a welcome relief to get out of the limelight and back to his pitch. He didn't miss the loss of the winning rosette so much as the absence of Ben. He'd made sure Ben would come. He'd searched the ringside as well as he could, but the one face he was anxious to see was missing. Perhaps he was late and would come over to the pitch, but as the afternoon wore on and the only people who came were the children for rides, Joe realised that Ben wasn't coming at all.

He didn't see Nina either. He thought she'd want to watch the ponies jumping, but she must have had other things to do, unless she was somewhere around the crowded ring and would be coming across before tea. But no one came except customers and these had dribbled to nothing by four o'clock.

At four-fifteen, just as Mr Hawton had promised, his son Jeremy arrived to relieve Joe for a cup of tea. There was not much trade, but Joe handed over the eight shillings he'd taken in case Jeremy needed the change. The boy was younger than Joe, with a shock of ginger hair and a slight stutter, but he seemed bright enough to handle the job. He didn't know much about donkeys (he was keen on butterflies), but he said he'd look after Smokey.

While Joe had a cup of tea and a fruit bun in the refreshment tent the gymkhana came to an end and a few minutes later the speakers announced the Sultan and his Fire Eaters. Joe finished his tea quickly. He'd like to see them. He knew the army motor cycle display was the finale, and followed the Sultan. He'd have to be back with Smokey when the engines roared. But he didn't see why he couldn't pinch a few minutes off to see the fire eaters.

The crowds were so thick around the section of the ring where the Sultan was to perform, Joe reckoned the flower show tents must be empty. He perched himself on a heap of straw bales at the back of the audience and just managed to see over the heads. A hastily erected tent stood a few yards across the ring, and a girl and man appeared in brief oriental clothes. They carried a flaming torch in each hand and sank to their knees, bowing their heads towards the tent entrance. The flaps suddenly parted and the Sultan stood there. He wore trunks too, and the turban on his head had a sparkling stone and sprouted a silver feather. He had a big red chest and long, hairless legs and muscles for arms which he folded over his chest.

Everyone waited, tense and quiet, for the Sultan to make a move. He stood for a moment just for the effect, then suddenly barked an order. Instantly, his worshippers raised their heads and threw their flaming torches to him. One at a time, of course, but very quickly. He began to run the flames over his body and legs and then taking one torch in his right hand he held it high, tipped back his head and opened his big mouth. Just when he was going to eat the fire, Joe felt something pull at his leg.

He glanced down, shocked to see Jeremy. Jeremy looked shocked as well.

'J-Joe,' he stuttered. 'Your donkey's—g-gone!'

'*What?*' All his breath was in the question.

'He's—g-gone!' Jeremy repeated miserably.

Joe reached the ground and his knees were shaking.

'*Gone?* What're you talking about? Gone

where? How did you let him go? What happened?'

Jeremy seemed overwhelmed.

'It was some b-big b-boys,' he said. 'One wanted a ride and he p-paid his m-money, b-but Smokey wouldn't g-go.'

'Yes,' said Joe, impatiently. 'Yes—then what happened?'

'One of the other b-boys—t-townies they were—pulled a bunch of n-nettles and whacked his b-behind. And—S-Smokey b-b-bolted.'

Joe was pale with anger and anxiety. He didn't know what to do first. He wished he'd got Ben to help him. He looked around for a policeman, but P.C Fowler was on his way to the gate, ready to see the traffic out, and the sergeant and inspector were in the secretary's tent having a quiet drink.

'Where did you last see him?' Joe turned to Jeremy.

'He f-followed the p-pitch as f-far as the g-gap in the hedge. The b-boy fell off and they all ran away.'

'But which way did Smokey go?'

'Well—' Jeremy scratched his head and blinked. 'He w-went one side of the he-hedge, then the other, and I wasn't s-sure—'

'How long ago?' Joe interrupted.

'A f-few minutes. I ran s-straight to the refreshment t-tent. Then I saw you on the s-straw.'

Joe gave him a handful of sugar cubes. 'We'll have to split up. We've got to find him. He might be hurt.'

'I th-think he was all right.'

'You only *think*.' Joe glanced around again. 'Goodness knows where he is in this lot.' He gripped Jeremy's arm, and pointed. 'You go that way, the other side of the ring and out to the enclosure. He might be amongst the other animals.'

Jeremy nodded solemnly.

'If you find him, coax him with the sugar and take him to the pitch. Hold him tight and wait by the horse-box.'

Jeremy said he'd do that, and they quickly parted company.

Joe began to run, his heart already pounding. Where was he going to start?... The back of the refreshment tent...Smokey might be hungry and the scent might have led him there. But all he could see behind the tent was a provision van and empty crates. He hurried to the boundary hedge and crawled through a gap to the road. There was nothing to be seen. Some people, a few cars. That was all.

Inside the meadow again he made for the water tanks at the back of the marquee. No sign of Smokey there. He could hear the army motor bikes warming up now, getting ready for the act. Joe was so afraid the noise would scare Smokey even more, wherever he was. And he just had to find him before it was dark. Already the sun was going down, the light was growing dull and a misty coolness was filling the air.

As he skirted the end marquee a woman running out stopped breathlessly to speak to a woman walking in. Joe caught a wisp of conversation...

'Have you see the tent stewards, Mildred?' asked the woman coming out.

'No, Edie, I haven't; but I 'spect they're watching the bikes in the ring.'

'Well, they'd better be seeing to their duties,' Edie said indignantly. 'There's a masterous mess in there. Fair shameful, it is. You never see such a riot as it's made o' the Miscellaneous.'

'What has?'

'A donkey.'

'What—in there?'

'And drunk it looks on Miss Gunston's gooseberry wine...'

Joe didn't stop for more. He knew Smokey was the culprit. He dashed into the tent.

It was a bit gloomy inside. There were only a couple of women, and one looked like Miss Gunston hurrying out of the side exit. Half-way along, the bit tent was partially divided by canvas screening separating the Miscellaneous from the flower classes. There was no sign of Smokey in the first half, and as he hurried by the trestle table displaying the home-made wine Joe saw the empty bottle lying on its side with the First Prize ticket underneath. The table was saturated, and several other exhibits lay about in disarray.

The woman stared, white faced, at Joe.

'It was a donkey,' she said. 'Rubbed against the table and knocked over Miss Gunston's wine. The judges left the cork out. The donkey was drinking it.' She glanced at the exit. 'They've gone for the stewards.'

'Where's the donkey now?' Joe demanded hoarsely.

The woman nodded fearfully towards the decorative section. 'In there, it went. D'you think you can get it?'

'I hope so,' Joe muttered fervently, and as he ran forward his foot caught some object below the tables. A soft, spongy object, like a flabby football. He bent and picked it up, and a First Prize card fell away underneath. It was the remains of a cake. Mrs Potter's honey cake.

He dreaded the thought of what was to come, but the last thing he thought of was Mrs Chester-Smyth. She must have just arrived, her husband at her heels, and was hurrying to the far corner of the tent. Joe stood and gaped across the neat tables of flowers as far as the disordered corner. Smokey was there, amidst a mess of table tops and trestles with pot blooms and vases at his feet. A small crowd, half-surrounding him, were trying to coax him into the aisle.

Mrs Chester-Smyth had stopped dead in her tracks and now threw up her hands in horror. Joe thought she was going to have hysterics as she turned on her husband.

'Gerald!' she shrieked. 'Do something, Gerald! It's ruined my prize begonia!'

Gerald did something. He pushed his way through the crowd and whacked Smokey across the rump with the flat handle of his shooting stick. The donkey

189

reared up, and the crowd fell back, and with his hind legs flying, Smokey roared out of the tent.

It was over in seconds and Joe hadn't moved. Now he swung round quickly, unable to face the crowd, and ran back the way he'd come.

Outside the ground, he was bewildered again. He didn't know which way to turn, until he heard the motor bikes and the shouting round the ring. He managed to push his way through almost to the ropes.

The army team were riding eight bikes abreast, their team-mates standing on each other's shoulders, to form a human pyramid. The man at the top was three men high and made a thrilling spectacle; but what horrified Joe was Smokey standing dazedly like a target in the middle of the ring.

Joe tried to struggle forward, but he was tightly wedged in between two hefty farm workers who thought the donkey was part of the act. Almost suffocating, he was forced to look on, the perspiration running down his face.

The stewards were in the ring now. They ran towards Smokey while the army turned slowly to one side. But the stewards, in their haste, confused Smokey even more and he ran in the wrong direction...straight across the riders' path. The line wobbled and split, and four machines peeled to the left and four to the right; and as the pyramid collapsed, Smokey turned and ran through the middle, and out the other side.

Joe thrust and pushed and backed his way out. He had that awful sensation in the stomach when you feel your heart's been in your mouth. The fiasco in the tent was bad enough, but this capped the lot. Smokey might have been killed. But no one had been hurt in the mêlée. Smokey was the only casualty because he was still missing, and as Joe surveyed the ground he realised he was back where he started.

It was not until the show was closing and the fair was opening with its lights and music that Joe and Smokey came together again. He found the donkey hiding in the horse-box when he finally went back to the pitch. The animal seemed tired and dusty, and Joe wondered if he was hurt. He couldn't be sure in the shadowy light of the horse-box but wild horses wouldn't have dragged Smokey on to the showground again.

Jeremy came over, relieved to see Smokey, and took the water pail his father had left; when he had gone Joe settled down on the ramp to wait.

It was getting dark when the groom arrived. Although he hadn't been at the show he'd heard a lot about it.

'Believe you had quite a rumpus in the flower show tent,' he declared as Joe helped him raise the tailboard of the horse-box. 'Seems one o' the donkeys went on the randy and made a fine old mess of some exhibits.' He chuckled in the dark. 'Mrs Chester-Smyth blew her top, I hear. That must have been a sight—did you see it?'

'Not all of it,' Joe murmured.

'Then didn't the li'l varmint play havoc in the ring?'

'There was some trouble there.'

'Quite a lively turn-out altogether, I reckon.'

'Yes,' Joe said faintly. 'I believe it was.' He was thinking about Mrs Chester-Smyth. 'I hope there wasn't much damage or the people too upset.'

'The Guv'nor sugared 'em over. You

can trust the Colonel to do that. Blooming diplomat, he is.' He glanced down. 'Did you have any luck, Joe?'

'No. No luck at all.'

'Well, we can't all win,' the groom said cheerfully. He nodded at the box as he shot the bolts of the tailboard. 'Your beast seems quiet. Run off his feet, I s'ppose?'

Joe pulled a wisp of straw from his ear.

'Yes,' he said. He's had quite a busy day.'

Joe was glad to get home to Valley End. He'd intended going back on his bike to the fair, but he was feeling too tired. What's more, he didn't like the look of Smokey. Even when he'd brushed him gently down, his coat still looked rough and dirty, and there was a peculiar, dazed sort of air about him as if he was sickening for something. Of course, it might have been the gooseberry wine or something he'd eaten. Then look what he'd been through! No wonder he didn't look well. Who would? Joe offered him some water and tried a little mash, but Smokey only turned his head away. And Joe didn't like it at all. He thought he'd better tell Mrs Massiter.

193

But she was in bed when he got into the house. She was feeling much better and had been up all afternoon, but when Mr Massiter arrived he thought she shouldn't take any risks. So after Mrs Potter had brought home the prizes and reported the scenes, Mrs Massiter went back to bed.

Mr Massiter looked very fit with his Caribbean tan, and had driven himself down from London Airport in the Rolls. He was very nice to Joe when he heard the boy was worried about Smokey, though Joe didn't explain about the shocks of the afternoon. Mr Massiter went over to the stable to see the patient for himself, and after due consideration it was decided to call the vet.

It seemed a miserably long time between the 'phone call and his arrival, but Smokey didn't appear any worse. The vet was very thorough. He took Smokey's temperature and prodded him in the stomach and looked in his mouth. Then he gave him an injection.

'Nothing organic,' murmured the vet. 'Just a little bit overstrained, I'd say.' He looked at Joe. 'What's he been doing to-day?'

'Quite a lot,' Joe said. 'And he drank

194

some gooseberry wine.'

The vet didn't seem surprised. He liked gooseberry wine himself. His mother used to make it.

'He'll be all right,' he said confidently. 'Right as rain in forty-eight hours. Don't worry about the food. Just give him water when he wants it. Let him have a little walk to-morrow.'

Joe said he'd do all that.

The vet closed his bag, nodded to Mr Massiter who'd been standing in the background all the time, and stepped outside.

'I'll look in again on Monday,' he said with a final glance at Smokey. 'Meantime, just keep an eye on him.'

Joe kept an eye on him, even though Smokey was much better Sunday morning. Joe didn't go to church with the Massiters and Mrs Potter because of his nursing duties. He didn't go over to Ben's either, though he wanted to see him to relate all that had happened on Saturday. He just stayed put, following the vet's advice, and you'd never believe the difference on Monday. The old lustre was back in Smokey's eyes and he waggled his ears when Joe wished him good morning.

He'd got his appetite back, too, but Joe didn't think he'd better take him on to the paddock till the vet had been.

Although Mrs Massiter had been fine on Sunday, she was a bit off colour again on Monday morning, so Mr Massiter rang his specialist in London. An appointment was arranged for eleven a.m on Tuesday, and as the wisest course was to spend the night in town, they drove off in the Rolls after lunch.

The vet arrived in the late afternoon, and one look at Smokey was enough. Joe was very relieved, though he'd expected the result, and as soon as the man had gone he took the donkey out to the paddock for an hour.

Towards the end of the afternoon Joe set off on his bike to Ben's place *en route* for the fair. Despite his relief and sense of freedom, he was a little concerned about Mrs Massiter. She didn't look as if she had much wrong—just a bit tired, perhaps. And everyone got a bit tired sometimes. The specialist would probably give her a tonic, like the one Mr Massiter had. Maybe that's all she needed. He didn't think there was really anything to worry about.

With the Massiters away and the Potters

back at Valley End for the night, Joe felt free to spend a long evening at the fair. He had a lot to make up for not going back there on Saturday night. He wanted a go at the Dodg'ems, to see the chimps and to return Nina's lucky charm. If Saturday was a demonstration of the kind of luck it brought, she was welcome to keep it.

Ben was not at home when Joe reached the cottage. He rode his bike round to the back. The door was locked, and although the key was in the privy, as usual, he decided not to go in. There was no point in waiting and as it looked as if the hens had recently been fed, Ben might not be back till late. He'd pop over again to-morrow. He wanted to get to the fair.

When he biked on to the ground he saw that all the show tents had gone, and the fair had the meadow to itself. In the dusk of early evening it looked like some magic island of light vibrant with music and life.

Already the avenues between the coloured stalls were thronged with people, the amusements were building up to full swing. The grand roundabout with its galloping horses was a giant centrepiece of gilt and glitter and music in the brilliant lights. The Dodg'ems were moving, the Chair-o-planes flying, the swings rocking. Skittles were cracking, guns were popping, the hoop-la and the bingo stalls were in full cry. The shouts and shrieks and laughter rallied and fell with the blare and grind of the organ music.

Joe hid his bike in the hedge and started his tour round, and just as he reached the Steeds' big tent Nina came out.

'Joe!' she called, and ran to meet him. 'I was wondering when you'd come. What happened to you Saturday night?'

'What happened to *you* in the afternoon?' he countered. 'I didn't see you at the races.'

She pulled a face. 'No. But I didn't mean to miss them. It was such a nuisance. I had to go in to Lotchford with Daddy to get some shopping, and the radiator played up again. He had to have a new one fitted and we didn't get back till the afternoon. But I went to the show and looked round the ring. Didn't see you.' She looked at him. 'How did it go?'

'Awful,' he said, and told her the whole story.

Nina had to laugh when he told her about the fiasco in the tent and the trouble in the ring, but she agreed it was serious really.

'So we took Smokey straight home,' he ended. 'That's why I didn't come back.'

'Poor Smokey,' she murmured, and her eyes were misty with sympathy. 'But he's quite better now?'

'Yes, as right as rain.' Joe was looking up at the coloured board announcing *Steed's Famous Chimps* over the entrance to the tent. 'I've come to see the tea party,' he said.

'They're just finishing the act,' she explained. 'It'll be half an hour yet before the next performance. We'll come back then.'

'Come back?'

She nodded, smiling. 'I want to go on the Ghost Train.'

They went on the Ghost Train; and the Chair-o-planes; the Roundabout; and the Dive-Bomber. And when it came to paying, Joe paid. She wanted to treat him, too. But he wouldn't let her. Mr Massiter had given him a pound. And when he'd settled the argument, they went on the Dodg'ems.

The traffic was pretty heavy, every car was engaged; but Joe noticed that Charlie wasn't there. When the man taking the money jumped on the back of their car, Joe asked him where Charlie was.

'Charlie Oldham, you mean?' the man growled. 'Ask me another. He's never around when there's work to do. Ain't seen him to-day at all.'

They stayed in the car another two rounds, and when they left the rink, Nina had forgotten to ask Joe about Charlie. She was more interested in things nearer home.

'You're good on the Dodg'ems, Joe,' she said, her face glowing with the action and excitement. 'You going to be a racing driver when you grow up?'

'No.'

'But you'd be famous.'

'I'd rather be happy.'

'They go together.'

'I don't reckon so. Not always.'

Nina pouted and blinked her long lashes. 'Well, I'm going to be famous.'

'You're different.'

'Everybody has a chance to be famous. But I suppose it's easier for a dancer. A ballet dancer. That's what I'm going to be.' They were moving slowly through the fringe of the sideshows. Nina glanced at him shyly. 'What are you going to be, Joe?'

'Something to do with animals is what I want. Like Ben.'

'Ben? Who's he?'

'He's my friend. He's been—well, like a guide really. All I know about the country here, and the wild creatures living in it, is all because of him.'

'Where does he live?'

'Oh—in a cottage.'

'How does he get money, then?'

'He doesn't bother much about money. He keeps a few hens. Helps on the farm. Things like that.'

Nina turned up her pretty nose.

'Well, that doesn't sound like working with animals,' she said. 'I mean, proper animals. Now, if that's what you want, Joe, you ought to work for Daddy. He's having more animals next season.'

'He is? What—more monkeys?'

'Well—I'm not sure if he's going in for more chimps or whether he's going to change the act. Mummy's talked about sea-lions. But I don't know what they'll end up with.'

Joe stopped and faced her.

'But if he wants help,' he said, 'why

don't you help him instead of going in for dancing? Don't you like animals?'

She laughed. 'I love them. But I love dancing, too. I'm going to a proper ballet school next term. My dancing mistress says I've got natural talents.'

'I s'ppose she should know.' He was watching the queue filing into her father's tent.

Nina suddenly stepped back and up on to her toes. She pirouetted a couple of times.

'Would you like to see me dance, Joe?' she smiled.

'No. Not now,' he said. 'I'd like to see the chimps.'

It was late when he got back to Valley End; later than usual. Joe put away his bike and went quickly towards the lobby door. He could see the lighted kitchen window and guessed the Potters were there. He wouldn't disturb them. Mrs Potter would only make a fuss. So he'd just call good night and go straight to his room.

The kitchen window was still open, and when he passed he could see them sitting over their bed-time coffee. Mrs Potter was talking, but Joe wasn't listening as he felt for the handle of the lobby door. His fingers closed on the handle, but he didn't turn it. It was Mr Potter's voice in the kitchen that seemed to freeze everything outside.

'Bit risky, isn't it, Emily, at Mrs Massiter's age?' The question seemed to shatter the night scented air, although it was spoken in mild enough tones.

'She's not so old.' Mrs Potter was speaking. 'Well the right side of forty. Besides, she's had a child before.'

'I didn't know that.'

'No reason why you should, Daniel Potter. She told me once. It was many years ago—a boy, died in infancy. So what more natural, I say, now that they've come together again.'

Joe still couldn't move. Only their words were moving—registering in his brain.

'Did she tell you, then? About it this time?' Mr Potter asked.

'No, she wouldn't say anything. Don't s'ppose she believes it's possible.' There was the clatter of a cup and saucer. 'But I reckon she's on the way. Had my suspicions when she was queer on Saturday morning.'

'Dear me,' Mr Potter clicked his tongue.

'I wondered why he was so keen to get her to a specialist when she didn't seem to be ill. I suppose they *will* go back to London now?'

'That'll be the next move, for sure,' said Mrs Potter thoughtfully.

'What about the boy then, and his donkey?'

There was a momentary pause as if Mrs Potter might have been shrugging her shoulders.

'The boy'll go away to college, I s'ppose,' she said. 'Gawd knows what they'll do with the donkey.'

CHAPTER 11

Joe had made up his mind by the morning. All night long he'd tossed and turned, his pillow damp where the tears had been. If he closed his eyes the nightmare got worse. It was better to keep awake. Keeping awake helped to separate dream from reality. Gave him time to sort things out. And when daylight came, he knew what he must do.

It was no use crying. Only girls cried. And he was ashamed of himself for behaving like one. He'd got to grow up. Stand on his own feet. That's what Uncle Bert had said. Now he knew what he must do he could tell them straight. Tell them nicely. But let them see he'd made up his mind. They were going to do what they wanted. Surely he had a choice?

Mrs Massiter was going to live a different life now. She'd have her own family again. They were going back to London, to the house in Regent's Park. Of course, she'd say it wouldn't make any difference. That's what she always said. What an empty promise it was! Everything made a difference. But she couldn't help that. She'd meant every word when she'd said it. He didn't want to upset her. She'd been so kind. It was *her* happiness. And she deserved to have it back again.

Joe took the short cut across Prospect Meadow to Winkletye Lane. He wanted to walk to Ben's place. It gave him time to plan what he would say. After all the chatter with the Potters because he couldn't eat much breakfast, he was relieved to get away where he could think again... Think about his plan...

He'd put it gently to Ben. He'd keep very calm. As calm as Ben always was. They were so much alike, he'd say. Got on so well together. He didn't want to leave the valley. He didn't want to leave Ben. He couldn't leave Smokey. There must be something they could do. And he'd thought of a way... There was a spare room at the cottage. He was sure Mrs Massiter would pay the rent, and he could do odd jobs about the place. In the garden and with the fowls. And when he left school, well—he could work on a farm. Perhaps Brierley's would have him. He wouldn't be in the way. Surely Ben could see how easy it would be. He would understand. You could always rely on Ben...

But when Joe reached the cottage Ben wasn't there. The door was locked, but the key wasn't in the privy. He mooched around the garden, saw the hens had been fed. There was nothing he could do except wait. He sat down on the elm stump and watched the time go by. The morning drifted slowly away and although it was warm in the sun, Joe could sense the touch of autumn in the air. The garden had that empty, end-of-summer look that took all the green colour away.

Joe hadn't a watch but he could tell the time by the sun, and knew he ought to go back to lunch. He didn't want to leave but Mrs Potter would only start asking questions if he didn't show up. He began the rounds again. The packing-shed, the garden, and circled the house, but still Ben didn't come. He stood, miserable, on the rough brick path. It was an effort to keep cheerful when you were wondering where your friend was, but it was no good waiting any longer. He'd have to come back that afternoon.

He felt better after lunch. And the cottage door was open when he got there. But things didn't seem the same inside. Ben's pipe lay broken on the kitchen table and the broom cupboard door gaped wide, all the familiar things in it disturbed. The small dresser cupboard lay open, the one in which Ben had found the rum. Now all the contents were strewn on the coconut matting. The door to the passage stood ajar. Joe moved back and turned apprehensively towards it as footsteps descended the stairs.

He wasn't sure who he expected to see, but was shocked to find it was Fowler.

'I—I called to see Ben,' Joe said. His voice sounded weak and a long way off.

'I know.' P.C Fowler stepped into the room and put his helmet on the table. 'It's very hard to have to tell you, Joe.' His voice was warm and kind. 'But you'd find out sooner or later.'

Joe didn't understand. He stared at the man. His mouth was dry, his tongue like a wedge of blotting paper.

'Find out?'

Fowler put a hand on the boy's shoulder.

'Listen, laddie,' he said. 'Sometimes it's hard to understand what people do. Why they do it. We never get to know them, however close we are. They live a life on the surface that everyone can respect. But underneath they're quite a different being. Then one day, they overdo it, and they're found out for what they are.'

'What d'you mean, sir?' Joe was bewildered. 'Where *is* Ben?'

'Over at Lotchford.'

'Is—that where he was this morning? And last night too?'

Fowler nodded slowly.

'D'you mean he hasn't been here at all?'

The policeman nodded again.

'Then who's feeding the fowls?'

'A man from the farm. The sergeant got on to Brierley.'

The sergeant....Lotchford...Joe could only think of accidents.

'You see, Joe,' Fowler said gently, 'Ben Pollard's been arrested.'

Joe hadn't dreamed of that. He couldn't believe it. He *was* dreaming. No one would arrest Ben. He stared at the fatherly figure in uniform. He wanted to say something, but nothing would come.

'I'm afraid we've been checking on him for some time, Joe. Ever since, in fact, that morning the sergeant and I met you here. But we had no proof then.'

Joe still couldn't say anything. But he remembered it all. He thought the trouble was the broken window at *The Crown*. And Ben let him believe it.

'They're holding him over at Lotchford,' Fowler's voice went on. 'Along with a man named Charlie Oldham.'

The name sank in. He remembered seeing Charlie that day, too. A customer Ben had called him. Charlie said he had connections. Joe began to see what kind of connections they were now. He wasn't at the fair last night... He was with Ben...

'What have they done?

'More than enough to earn them a sentence,' Fowler said. 'They were caught red-handed last night on the Darren Hall estate. They had a large bag of ducks in Oldham's van.'

'I don't believe it!'

Fowler shook his head and glanced significantly round the kitchen.

'We had a warrant to search the cottage,' he explained. 'The C.I.D sergeant from Lotchford has only just gone.'

Joe stared at the broken pipe, the littered floor—yet, still he couldn't accept it.

'Not Ben!' he whispered.

'I knew it would come hard, laddie.' Fowler moved back towards the door. 'But just come upstairs and you can see for yourself.'

Still in a daze, Joe followed him to Ben's bedroom. The door in the wall was open. The door that had been locked the day he'd released the sparrow. Joe stood in the middle of the room, staring at the narrow gap, which the policeman filled.

'Come in and see,' Fowler invited, and moved into the little room.

Joe went in and saw. Larry had been right. Ben was a poacher. All the tools of the trade were there. The two guns in the wall rack, the open chest on the floor. The snares, the decoy net, even the dreaded gin-trap, hammered home the truth of all Fowler's statements. For Joe's sake Ben had lived a lie. He didn't really care for the things Joe held dear; he simply turned them into money. That's the way the mallard ducks had gone. Joe could see that now. He had never seen them fly. Ben would have clipped their wings, and taken them when they were ready. He found his markets through Charlie, and the garden produce was a sideline compared to the game in Marley Wood and the fields surrounding it. Charlie must have led him on. And now had come the final shame that had brought him to the end of the line. But why—why had he lived the lie for Joe? What reason had he for pretending?

Joe didn't realise he'd spoken the last thought aloud until he heard Fowler attempt to answer.

'I don't know, laddie. It's hard to tell what someone's motives are. But I think he was a lonely man.' He paused. 'He had a boy once. That photo by his bed. I think you reminded him of his son.'

'That's no excuse for pretending, for leading me on,' Joe struggled to hold back the tears. 'He could have sent me away the first day I came. That's what a man would have done.' He remembered the day. The scene in the hen runs. The panicking hens flapping over the garden. Ben had told him a fox had been in and broken down the netting. Joe had helped to catch the fowls and afterwards they'd sat and talked. Joe had told him of his life and the animals he had brought from Sparrow Street.

'Perhaps he would have sent you away, Joe, if he hadn't got to know you.' Fowler broke into his thoughts. 'You see, he lost his son in an accident. Perhaps he had to go on pretending for fear of losing you.' He glanced reflectively at the window. The last butterfly of summer was fluttering there. 'Who knows, maybe he meant to tell you one day. When you were old enough to learn that a man is not always what he seems to be.'

Joe closed his eyes, to shut out the scene. It seemed the end of the world for him.

'You put him on a pedestal, laddie.' Fowler shook his head sadly. 'And when you do that with a man there's always the risk that one day you'll discover he's only

212

a paper hero.' He put his arm round Joe's shoulder and together they went down to the kitchen. 'He'll be as upset as you are when he knows you know the truth. You don't want to see him—if it could be arranged?'

Joe shook his head.

'No,' he said. 'I don't want to see him now.'

It seemed to take a long time for the numb feeling to go. He walked in all directions on the way back to Valley End. There was nothing to look forward to now. Nowhere to go. No one to turn to. There was only Smokey left. He was his only friend.

Dusk was drawing its shadow across the sky when Joe reached the house. He went straight to the paddock. He found Smokey at the gate, waiting for his evening meal. Joe put his arm round the donkey's neck, and gazed sadly over the valley.

The fair was coming to life. The lights were a gay contrast to his sombre mood. And the music started to play. Smokey seemed to hear and nudged Joe's jacket. But he only wanted a lump of sugar. Joe felt in his pocket and his fingers closed on Nina's lucky charm. He'd forgotten to give it back to her. But she meant him to keep it. Perhaps he should... His eyes focused on the lights once more. The music seemed to call across the valley... Perhaps Nina's lucky charm would bring him some luck after all...

CHAPTER 12

Laura Massiter found the note when they got back from London. In her bedroom, it was. Propped against her powder bowl on the dressing-table.

She ran back on to the landing, the square of paper trembling in her fingers, and called down the stairs.

'He's gone, Arnold!' she cried. 'He's gone!'

'Who's gone?' He spoke a little testily as he came out of the lounge. He'd just poured a drink, and his rather hectic West Indies' trip, and the drives to and from town, had taken the go out of him a bit. He looked up the stairs. 'Who's gone, Laura? If you're talking about the Potters, I told them they could go.'

x

She shook her head and came running downstairs until the sudden ring of the telephone bell jerked her to a halt. She stared at the instrument, her knuckles white on the banister rail, as he crossed the hall to answer it.

He looked up at her, his hand covering the mouthpiece.

'It's Rawlins,' he said softly.

She made no movement; just watched him, listening, as he spoke. 'I'm delighted to hear that... It's splendid news... Yes...I will... Of course...' He replaced the 'phone and came back to the stairs. 'It's the reservoir,' he said. 'Rawlins has won his battle. The valley's saved. They've settled for the Wyanstone site after all.'

She came down then, but it was as if she hadn't heard.

'Aren't you pleased?' he asked, taking her hand. Then he saw the square of paper. But still her manner puzzled him.

'Didn't you hear?' she blurted. 'Joe's gone!'

'Gone where?'

'To the fair.'

'Well, it's nothing to get het-up about. It's the last night. I'm not surprised—'

'Read it, Arnold.' She thrust the paper

215

at him. 'Don't you see? He's gone—for *good!*'

His face paled. It had taken some moments to get the message. Now the shock had registered. He'd never considered the thought of Joe running away. Anxiously, he read it through, his eyes lingering over the most telling phrases...*And all the time Ben was pretending...I don't want to see him again... You're going back to London... You're sending me away to school... I can't leave Smokey... And I've no one in the valley now... So I'm going with the fair... It's best for all of us... Thank you for all the treats and kindnesses I've always had from you... I'll miss you... But if you have a son he'll make up for me...*

The last phrase held him fast. He read it again.

'What's he mean—a son? Where on earth did he get that idea?'

'What differences does it make now? We've lost Joe!'

'Nonsense. Laura, darling, be sensible. Don't get yourself worked up.' He struggled to disguise his own shocked feelings in the reassuring tenderness of his voice. 'I know it'll be all right.' He waved the paper. 'This is just a mood. He's stunned and distraught about Pollard, whatever the wretched man's done. And—from somewhere—God knows where—he's got this mistaken impression—about us. Of course, he's upset. But he'll be back.'

'He won't,' she whimpered. 'I know he won't. He means it.'

'Of course he does, for the moment. That's all. He's just a boy. He's got to learn. Let's wait and see. If he's not back to-night, I'll go and get him in the morning.'

'The fair will be gone in the morning. And he'll go with them. I know it. If he's taken Smokey—I know he won't come back. And don't you see? We haven't any legal claim to him. Oh—my God! We must go after him now.'

'Steady, Laura. Give the boy time to cool. He wouldn't come back this very minute if we went for him. But he'll be back by the morning.' He put his hand on her arm, but she threw it aside.

'Not if he's taken Smokey, I tell you.' She ran out of the door and across the drive.

The twilight was deepening, its shadow was everywhere. But she could see the stable door standing wide. Knew the stable was empty. She ran on, stumbling blindly towards the paddock. She could hear the music of the fair now. Loud and clear, high and low, rising and falling in the still air of the valley.

She threw her arms over the paddock gate, hugging it to her, and stared at the empty meadow. The lights of the fair flickered and danced as if keeping time with the music... Joe would come back. He must come back. He didn't belong at the fair... The lights across the valley danced before her eyes but soon they were a blur through the tears; and the bump and grind of the organ music seemed to fill the meadow.

The publishers hope that this book has given you enjoyable reading. Large Print Books are especially designed to be as easy to see and hold as possible. If you wish a complete list of our books, please ask at your local library or write directly to: Dales Large Print Books, Long Preston, North Yorkshire, BD23 4ND, England.

This Large Print Book for the Partially sighted, who cannot read normal print, is published under the auspices of

THE ULVERSCROFT FOUNDATION

THE ULVERSCROFT FOUNDATION

. . . we hope that you have enjoyed this Large Print Book. Please think for a moment about those people who have worse eyesight problems than you . . . and are unable to even read or enjoy Large Print, without great difficulty.

You can help them by sending a donation, large or small to:

**The Ulverscroft Foundation,
1, The Green, Bradgate Road,
Anstey, Leicestershire, LE7 7FU,
England.**
or request a copy of our brochure for more details.

The Foundation will use all your help to assist those people who are handicapped by various sight problems and need special attention.

Thank you very much for your help.